ID

"Do my love scenes...bother you for some reason?"

She studied the hard set of his mouth, intrigued. He'd acted almost *jealous*. The prospect tantalized her.

"Why should they? None of my business."

"It just seemed like...you were upset. You tensed up." She smoothed a hand along the taut, corded muscles of his arm, stroking her fingers to his fist to illustrate her point.

He rolled his shoulders as if trying to loosen the tension stringing him tight, then sighed a gush of breath. "All right, yes. It bothers me."

The corner of her cheek tugged up, and she playfully goaded, "Why?"

He jerked his head toward her. "Why?" he echoed, incredulous. "I— Hell."

His hazel eyes lasered down at her with breath-stealing intensity, and the air between them sparked and crackled. A low, frustrated growl rumbled from his throat, and a heartbeat later, his mouth descended on hers.

Dear Reader,

Working on continuities is always fun for me, and the Eden Falls Coltons were no exception. What fun it was to put tough guy Gunnar in charge of two energetic toddlers and bring the teasing, but always loving, Colton siblings to life. Imagining Violet's movie-star lifestyle was fun, too! Paparazzi, script changes, celebrity award shows…ah, the glamor! Yet I knew deep down she was a mother first and a down-to-earth Southern girl at heart.

Another fun twist? I had the pleasure of including my editor's cats in my story. It seemed the right thing to do, since the wise and wonderful Keyren Gerlach-Burgess created the continuity and loves cats as much as I do. She tells me the chicken theft incident really happened!

The peek into the Amish world was so interesting to me and brought back memories of traveling through Pennsylvania Dutch country with my family when I was a kid. I hope you'll love Gunnar and Violet's romance as much as I do, and come back next month for the next installment of the Coltons of Eden Falls!

Happy reading,

Beth Cornelison

Don't miss the other books in The Coltons of Eden Falls series:

COLTON DESTINY by Justine Davis

COLTON'S DEEP COVER by Elle Kennedy

COLTON SHOWDOWN by Marie Ferrarella

Colton's Ranch Refuge

BETH CORNELISON

First published in Great Britain 2013
by Mills & Boon, an imprint of Harlequin (UK) Limited.
Large Print edition 2013
Harlequin (UK) Limited,
Eton House, 18-24 Paradise Road,
Richmond, Surrey TW9 1SR   **LP**

© Harlequin Books S.A. 2012

ISBN: 978 0 263 23806 8

Special thanks and acknowledgment to Beth Cornelison for her contribution to The Coltons of Eden Falls miniseries.

Printed and bound in Great Britain
by CPI Antony Rowe, Chippenham, Wiltshire

BETH CORNELISON

started writing stories as a child when she penned a tale about the adventures of her cat, Ajax. A Georgia native, she received her bachelor's degree in public relations from the University of Georgia. After working in public relations for a little more than a year, she moved with her husband to Louisiana, where she decided to pursue her love of writing fiction.

Since that first time, Beth has written many more stories of adventure and romantic suspense and has won numerous honors for her work, including a coveted Golden Heart Award in romantic suspense from Romance Writers of America. She is active on the board of directors for the North Louisiana Storytellers and Authors of Romance (NOLA STARS) and loves reading, traveling, *Peanuts'* Snoopy and spending downtime with her family.

She writes from her home in Louisiana, where she lives with her husband, one son and two cats who think they are people. Beth loves to hear from her readers. You can write to her at P.O. Box 5418, Bossier City, LA 71171, or visit her website, www.bethcornelison.com

For Keyren—Thanks for the opportunity
to be part of Eden Falls!

Thank you to Jenni Nauright
and C.J. Lyons for all your help with
Violet's medical crisis and the proper
procedures for Amelia and Derek to take!
Any mistakes in this regard are mine.

Chapter 1

A chill November breeze buffeted Gunnar Colton's cheeks and sent a shiver rippling through him. Tension strung Gunnar as tight as a trip wire, and he cast a wary gaze around the downtown Eden Falls street. At first glance, nothing about the scene seemed amiss. Merchants decorated their shop windows for the upcoming holidays, and customers milled about casually enjoying the Saturday afternoon and hunting for early season bargains. Eden Falls was small-town Americana at its best, yet Gunnar couldn't relax, couldn't quiet the hum of anxiety buzzing through his veins.

"The cold air is making my nose run," sixteen-year-old Piper complained.

"Guess you better go chase it then," Sawyer teased.

Piper slanted her adopted brother a you're-so-stupid look before turning to Gunnar. "I'm freezing out here."

"So drink your hot chocolate. It'll warm you up." Gunnar curled his hands around his cocoa, soaking up the heat from the ceramic mug, and gave the teenager a patient glance.

She rolled her eyes and flopped back in her chair with a shake of her head.

The weather was too cold for them to be sitting outside, but Sawyer, Piper and Gunnar's eleven-year-old brother, had specifically requested that they drink their hot chocolate at the café's sidewalk table. Gunnar hadn't had the heart to tell Sawyer no, despite his own deeply personal reasons for being uneasy with the outdoor table. He felt exposed on the city street—jumpy, emotionally raw.

He turned his attention to the local street vendors selling holiday arts and crafts, and his mind wandered thousands of miles away....

The marketplace disintegrated into chaos as debris rained down on the street. Shouts and screams pierced the ringing in his ears as the concussion of the explosion echoed through the street.

"Gunnar? Did you hear me?" Piper asked, giving him a half worried, half exasperated frown.

"I'm sorry. What?"

"Can I go to Très Chic and look at their jeans while you two finish your cocoa?"

He shook his head. "Stay with us. We'll be done in a minute. Then we'll go with you."

Piper and Sawyer sent him matching looks of horror.

"To a girl's store?"

"Gunnar!"

He divided a look between his youngest siblings, knowing he was totally out of his league—what did an ex-soldier know about raising teenagers?—but determined to reconnect with his family after so many years away. Sawyer had been a baby when Gunnar had enlisted in the army and had left for his first tour of duty in Afghanistan. His brother felt like a stranger. And teenage Piper bore little resemblance to the sweet little sister he'd hugged goodbye eleven years ago.

"Listen, if you'll—"

The roar of a motorcycle engine yanked Gunnar's attention away midsentence. He jerked his gaze toward the black sport bike speeding toward them, and ice filled his veins.

The moped sped past them, breaching the security checkpoint and ramming into the crowded marketplace. Sam and Ronnie were on their feet in an instant. "Suicide bomber!"

Gunnar jolted as the bomb in his memory exploded with a deafening blast.

This motorcycle rider wore a backpack. He drove right up onto the sidewalk.

"Get down!" Gunnar grabbed the front of Sawyer's jacket and yanked him from his chair to the ground. In an instant, he'd shoved Piper to the sidewalk as well and flipped their table on its side to serve as a blast shield—as if the flimsy metal table was any real protection from a half dozen sticks of dynamite or a block of C-4.

With an arm around each of his startled siblings, Gunnar huddled behind the table, bracing for the fireball, the concussion, the chaos. His heart drummed a frantic tattoo against his ribs. Despite the cold, a film of sweat popped out on his forehead. Adrenaline sent a shudder rolling through him.

"Gunnar? Wh-what's wrong? Why are we hiding?" Sawyer asked.

Several seconds had passed with no explosion. Passersby on the sidewalk sent them curious looks and half-hidden grins behind gloved hands. Had the detonator failed? Had the bomber balked?

In the wake of the blast, he staggered to his feet, tasted blood in his mouth, searched the street for his friends, for the woman and her son...

Nausea churned in his gut, and he struggled

for a breath. It was still so fresh, so real, so terrifying.

Piper wiggled free of his grasp, shooting him
an annoyed yet troubled look. "What are you
doing?"

Gunnar dragged a shaky hand over his face,
blinking hard to separate the present from the
past. "The motorcycle. He had a backpack. I
thought…"

"Of course he had a backpack. That's how
most people carry their stuff on a motorcycle."
Piper dusted her hands and shook her head.
"Why'd you freak out over that?"

"I thought…" Gunnar rubbed the bridge of
his nose, his breathing still ragged and his pulse
racing.

Piper clambered to her feet and cast her gaze
down the street…and gasped. Quickly she
dropped back behind the protection of the overturned table, her pale blue eyes wide with horror.

Gunnar's pulse ramped higher. "What?"

"The guy on the motorcycle…it's Heath Hamilton!" She squeezed her eyes shut and groaned.

"Oh, God, please, don't let him have seen me. I will *die* if he finds out it was us behind this table! Heath is only the hottest guy at school."

"At least you didn't skin your knee," Sawyer said.

Gunnar shifted his attention to his little brother. "You're hurt?"

"Thanks to you." His brother's soulful brown eyes blazed with accusation. "What did you think? That the motorcycle was going to run over us? That he had a gun?"

He saw Sawyer's ripped jeans and bloody knee, and his chest tightened. "Bomb. I thought he had a bomb."

Sawyer wrinkled his nose. "Dude, this is America, not Afghanistan. That kind of stuff doesn't happen here."

Gunnar lightly ruffled his brother's hair, swallowing the reply that sprang to his tongue. *But it has. The 9/11 terrorists killed our parents.*

"Sorry, buddy. I just…" Gunnar fisted his hands and shoved the last whispers of nightmarish tremors down, locking them in a corner of his brain where he didn't have to face the memories. "Let's get you home so Derek can take a look at that knee, huh?"

As he climbed to his feet, Gunnar cast a sheepish side glance to Piper. Her returned gaze was wary, worried, shaken. "Sorry, Piper. I didn't mean to embarrass you."

She glanced back toward the parked motorcycle as she pushed to her feet. "No harm done. I don't think he saw us." She sighed. "I don't think Heath even knows I exist." She paused and scrunched her nose. "Are you all right? You're sweating and shaking and stuff."

Gunnar wiped his face on his coat sleeve. "I'm fine."

"Did you really think Heath had a bomb?" Piper tucked her Nordic-blond hair behind her ear and gave him a puzzled frown. "Why would Heath Hamilton want to bomb Main Street?"

Gunnar righted the table and picked up the broken pieces of their hot chocolate mugs. "I'm sure he wouldn't. My mistake." Clearing his throat, he divided a look between his disgruntled siblings. "Say, guys, don't mention this to Derek or Emma. Okay?"

Sawyer shrugged. "Whatever."

Piper was less easily convinced, and she narrowed a suspicious gaze on Gunnar as he tossed the shattered ceramic pieces in the nearest trash can. "Why not? Why don't you want them to know?"

He lifted a shoulder, which protested with a sharp ache. Apparently in his dive to the sidewalk he'd jammed the joint. "I just don't want them worrying about me. They've got enough on their minds with this new case regarding the missing Amish girls and Derek hiring new help for his office."

The door to the coffeehouse opened, and the manager stepped out to surveyed the mess Gunnar had created. "Are you folks all right?"

Piper's cheeks, already pink from the cold, reddened further. Sawyer rolled his eyes and started walking toward their Suburban.

Gunnar pulled out his wallet, peeled off a couple one hundred dollar bills and handed them to the manager. "Here. This should cover the damage. We're sorry for the disturbance."

Turning, he hustled to catch up with Sawyer, and while his wallet was out, he handed his little brother a hundred dollar bill as well. "Buy yourself some new jeans. Okay, buddy?"

Sawyer's eyes lit up. "Wow! Thanks, Gunnar."

Piper's jaw dropped, and she grunted. "You're bribing him?"

Gunnar shook his head. "He tore his jeans. He needs new ones."

His sister twisted her mouth speculatively. "I broke a nail. Do I get money for a manicure?"

Gunnar doled her a hundred dollars, as well. "Cunning."

"So are you really a billionaire, Gunnar?" Sawyer asked as they reached the family's SUV. "I heard Tate saying you, like, made some kind of killer investments that went crazy while you were deployed, and now you've got something like nine bazillion dollars."

Gunnar unlocked the driver's door and flipped the switch to unlock the rest of the SUV doors.

"I prefer not to discuss my financial business with an eleven year old."

"Come on, Sawyer," Piper said, settling on the front passenger seat. "If he had billions of dollars, why would he be living in that little cabin at the edge of the ranch property?"

"I don't know, Piper," Sawyer sniped. "Why aren't you living in the Amazon with all the other giant women?"

Piper turned to glare at her brother, and Gunnar gritted his teeth as he pulled into traffic. "Cut it out, Sawyer. It was a legitimate question. And I live in the cabin because I want to." He hesitated, studying the passing farmland and quaint homesteads of Pennsylvania Dutch country, and considered the simple lifestyle of the local Amish population. He wasn't all that different from the Amish in that respect. "The cabin is all I need. It's just what I need. I like the quiet, the scenery and the proximity to you two brats." He smiled to take the sting from his teasing. "I missed you guys while I was overseas."

Gunnar glanced in the rearview mirror in time

to see Sawyer poke his MP3 player earplugs in his ears and face the window.

Piper had her arms folded over her chest and a pucker of consternation denting her forehead.

He reached over to squeeze her knee. "Why the frown?"

She shrugged and then sighed. "Am I too tall for guys to like me?"

Gunnar shook his head. "Don't let Sawyer get to you."

She scoffed. "I don't. It's just…"

"Piper, look at me." Gunnar stopped the Suburban at the double gate to the Colton family ranch, the Double C, and Sawyer hopped out to open the gate without being asked.

Gunnar drilled his younger sister with a hard gaze. Her cornflower-blue eyes held the vulnerability of youth along with a keen intelligence beyond her years. Gunnar felt a rush of protectiveness for his sister. The Amish girls from Paradise Ridge who'd been kidnapped were about Piper's age.

"What?" she asked when he lapsed into silence for too long.

"You are perfect just as you are. And you are beautiful. I'm going to be busy fighting off all the boys who'll be beating down your door in the next few years."

She gave him a lopsided smile. "You have to say that. You're my brother."

Gunnar drove through the gate Sawyer had opened and shook his head. "I have to say it, because it's true. You are beautiful, and I'll bet you a new pair of jeans that Heath Hamilton not only knows who you are but is working up the courage to ask you out."

She snorted and laughed. "Yeah, right."

Sawyer climbed back in the SUV and leaned over the front seat. "What's with all the cars and buses and stuff?"

"Huh?" Gunnar looked through the windshield where Sawyer pointed. Sure enough, the driveway to the main ranch house was full of unfamiliar vehicles, and the side road to Gunnar's cabin was blocked by a large tour bus. Irritation prickled Gunnar. He hated having his privacy invaded, and from the looks of it, the ranch was under a full-scale assault.

Piper gasped and rocked forward in her seat. "No way!"

"What?" Gunnar and Sawyer asked at the same time.

The teenager pointed to the small cluster of people standing near the front door of the house, talking to their brother Derek. "See the woman in the green dress? The one with short blond hair?"

Gunnar spotted the woman in question. In a purely visceral reaction to the lady's feminine curves, a flash of heat swamped him, and his body hummed with lust. *Yeowsa.*

"What about her?" Sawyer asked.

"Don't you recognize her? That's Violet Chastain!"

Gunnar rolled up his palm. "Never heard of her."

Sawyer opened his door and jumped out, while Piper goggled at Gunnar. "Are you kidding? She was nominated for an Oscar this year for *The Journey Home*. *People* magazine voted her one of their most beautiful people this year. She's in town to film that new movie called *Wrongfully Accused*."

Gunnar cut the engine and stared through the window at the curvy blonde. "Doesn't ring a bell." But he had to agree with the staff of *People* magazine. Violet Chastain was a stunner.

"Geez, what rock have you been living under?"

Gunnar cut his sister a dry look. "An Afghan rock, until six months ago."

Piper winced, looking contrite. "Sorry. That came out wrong."

"Don't sweat it, kiddo. So I take it this Violet person is a big deal to the media?"

"Oh, yeah. The biggest." Piper turned her gaze to the gathering of people on the lawn and shook her head in wonder. "I can't believe that Violet Chastain, the hottest star in Hollywood, is at my house!"

Gunnar grunted and climbed out of the Suburban. "Yeah, and her huge-honking bus is blocking my driveway."

* * *

The sound of car doors slamming pulled Violet's attention from her director's discussion with the Double C's owner about the scenes the production crew wanted to film at the spacious ranch.

"Well, there's some of the family now," Dr. Derek Colton said. The handsome African American nodded toward the newly arrived SUV and grinned. "Before I sign off on this deal, I'd like their opinions. This is their home, too."

Violet turned to greet Derek's family, and her practiced smile faltered for a moment. The teenage girl crossing the yard was as fair featured as Derek was dark, and Violet blinked her surprise at the incongruity.

The doctor chuckled. "I see your surprise. They're my *adopted* brothers and sister. All of the Colton children were adopted, so we're something of an eclectic mix."

"So you are," Violet said, putting her meet-the-public smile back in place as the lovely blonde girl and a sandy-haired boy of ten or eleven trotted up with eager grins.

"OMG! You're Violet Chastain!" the girl gushed. "I love your movies!"

"Smooth, Piper," the boy said. "Try not to drool on her."

Derek thumped his younger brother lightly on the shoulder, then introduced the kids to Violet and the rest of the assembled movie crew.

"Nice to meet you, Sawyer, Piper." Violet and the other crew members shook their hands.

"You're back early," Derek called to the man who'd been driving the SUV.

The brawny man bringing up the rear met her gaze, and an unexpected tremor stirred deep inside her. Whether her gut reaction was good or bad, Violet couldn't say. Derek Colton's brother could have been responding to a casting call for a nightclub bouncer…if the producers were looking for someone who oozed sex appeal along with his intimidating glower. He stalked toward the assembled group with his stubbled jaw set, his broad shoulders squared and his sexy lips pulled in a taut frown.

Violet tore her gaze away from the brooding man and gave herself a mental shake. Why was she noticing the guy's lips? She never paid attention to a man's mouth unless he was playing opposite her in a scene and she was expected to kiss him. The odds that she'd ever kiss *this* scowling linebacker were so slim as to be laughable.

As the dangerously good-looking Colton brother approached like a brewing tempest, Violet had to call on all her cool reserves, the practiced composure she drew from when facing a horde of merciless paparazzi, to not take a step back when he stormed up.

"We decided to skip lunch," he told his brother, then sent a suspicious look around the group. "What's going on?"

"Gunnar, this is Mac Gremble, the director of *Wrongfully Accused,* the movie that's filming in the area. They're scouting the ranch to use in a few scenes."

Mac shook the bouncer wannabe's hand. Then Derek turned to her.

"And I guess I don't have to tell you who this is."

The older Colton brother's hazel gaze slid to her. "Only because Piper just told me." Though he offered his hand in greeting, he didn't smile, and Violet's mouth dried when his large fingers swallowed hers in a tight grip.

She forced a polite smile. "Not a fan of the movies...Gunnar, is it?"

"I just don't follow Hollywood hype." He dropped her hand and shoved his fingers in the pockets of his jeans. "That and I've been out of the country until about six months ago."

"Oh?" Violet tipped her head. "Where? Europe? Japan?"

His gaze narrowed. "Afghanistan." His tone was grave and held a note of challenge, as if he dared her to comment on his military status. Though startled by his gruff attitude, she opened her mouth to thank him for his service to the country but didn't get the chance before he aimed a thumb at her bus. "That your behemoth?"

Violet cut a quick glance to Mac and Dr. Colton, uncertain what to make of Gunnar's rudeness. "It's my dressing room when we're on location and my—"

"Well, your *dressing room* is blocking the road to my cabin. You'll have to move it."

Violet took umbrage with his hostile tone and straightened her spine, lifted her chin. She refused to let him bully her without cause.

"Gunnar," Derek growled. "What's your problem?"

"No, no." Violet raised a hand to intercede. "He's right. My bus is blocking the driveway, and I'd be happy to have my driver move it."

Gunnar arched a dark eyebrow, his scowl fixed on her. "Good." He pivoted to walk away.

"If—"

He stopped and faced her, his eyes narrowing with suspicion.

Nervous energy pumped through her, the kind of jitters she used to get before taking the stage or filming a difficult scene. Pressing a hand to the flutter in her belly, she met Gunnar's gaze with dredged up courage. "If you'll ask me." She paused to swallow. "Nicely."

Big brother Colton blinked his surprise and cocked his head as if uncertain he'd heard her correctly.

Gunnar's siblings chuckled, and Mac shifted his feet uneasily, probably worried about PR or something that Violet no longer cared about. Why should she care what the public thought of her if they gave so little disregard to her feelings, her needs? The speculation and insinuations that filled the media coverage after Adam's death still stung, and the invasion of her privacy while she was grieving infuriated her.

After glaring at her for a moment, Gunnar turned to Derek and huffed an impatient sigh. "When I got home in May, all I asked was that I be given privacy and quiet. Is it so much to ask that my home be a refuge while I decompress from the crap I had to deal with in Afghanistan?"

Decompress? Violet found his choice of words intriguing. If Gunnar was still wound tight because of his war experiences, no wonder he was acting like such an ogre.

"No, it's not," Derek returned, his expression calm.

"Yet you've invited a horde of strangers to bring their cameras and lights and *dressing rooms*—" he cut a meaningful glance at Violet "—onto the ranch for who knows how long. Hardly my idea of rest or privacy, Derek."

"Which is why I've told Mr. Gremble that your cabin and the woods around it are off-limits. Any filming they do will be in and around the main house." When Piper drew an excited breath, her eyes widening, Derek aimed a finger at her. "You have to promise to stay out of their way and respect the confidentiality agreement. You can't tell anyone they are filming here. We don't want the media or rubberneckers milling around here."

"I can't even tell my friends?" Piper asked, aghast. "But—"

"Not even your friends," Derek said.

"Especially not your friends," Sawyer added. "Talk about gossip central. TMZ has nothing on Tiffany and Amber."

Piper glared at Sawyer. "Shut up, twerp."

"You shut up, Amazon."

Groaning, Derek scrubbed both hands over his face.

Gunnar grabbed Sawyer by the back of the coat and pulled him away from Piper. "Both of you give it a rest. Why do you have to antagonize each other all the time? Sheesh."

Violet flashed a lopsided grin. "So...is this what I have to look forward to?"

"I promise you they're not always this bad," Derek said.

"Oh, I didn't mean them." Violet waved her hands in denial. "I meant when my boys get older."

"You have kids?" Gunnar asked in a tone that said he found it difficult to believe.

Violet faced him again, bemused by his attitude. "Eighteen-month-old twins. They're with their nanny…in my *dressing room*."

She shot him a look that dared him to comment on that fact.

Gunnar sent her an annoyed look. "Your kids are *here?*"

"Yes. In the bus, napping."

"With a nanny."

"Yeaaahhh," she said drawing out the word, warily. "Where else would they be while I'm working?"

"Oh, I don't know. Maybe with their *father?* Or don't you Hollywood types believe in raising your own children?" Gunnar crossed his arms over his chest and sent her a condescending look she itched to slap off his smug face.

Violet gaped at him, too stunned to answer right away. The reference to Adam landed a punch in her stomach and sucked the air from her lungs.

"Um, Gunnar…helloooo?" Piper said. "Sawyer and I have a nanny."

He shot his sister a quelling look. "That's different."

"How?" Piper returned.

"It just is."

Mac stepped into the breach, shouldering in between her and the loutish Colton. "Look, pal, I don't know what your beef is, but if you—"

Violet grabbed Mac's sleeve, and shaking herself from her momentary daze, she shoved her director out of the way. Planting herself toe-to-toe with Gunnar, she met his gaze with a steely glare. Even standing as tall as she could, he dwarfed her by over a foot, but she refused to let his size or his gruff manner intimidate her. "My husband is *dead,* you oaf! Not that you'd know that since you don't keep up with 'Hollywood hype.'"

She poked him in his broad, rock-hard chest. "And while I'm on location, I keep my children near me, in my *dressing room,* because there is nothing, *nothing* more important to me than my boys. I want to be a part of their lives and involved in raising them as much as possible with my filming schedule." Fisting her hands at her sides, she raised up on her toes and stuck her face as close to his as she could. "Or don't you military types believe in women having a career and earning an income to feed her family?"

Around them no one moved, and the only sounds Violet could hear were the pounding pulse in her ears and her own angry breaths sawing from her lungs. Gunnar's hazel eyes bore into hers, unflinching, piercing, until her belly quivered with that disturbing energy again.

Finally he unfolded his arms and clapped slowly, mockingly. "Bravo, Ms. Chastain. You are very convincing as the offended and protective young mother. Oscar-worthy performance, for sure."

Violet knocked his hands out of the way and crowded so close to him that her body bumped his muscled torso and sparks skittered through her veins. "You're an ass, Gunnar Colton."

He simply lifted a corner of his mouth in an aggravating grin and said in a cloyingly sweet tone, "Thanks, Tinkerbell. Now would you pretty please move your oversize dressing room from my driveway, so I can get to my cabin?"

Tinkerbell?

Violet held her ground, chewing the inside of her cheek and deciding her best response. This close to him, his body heat and pine scent surrounded her, teasing her senses, her ability to think going haywire.

"Oh. My. God!" Piper groaned. "Enough with the foreplay. Would you two just get a room already?"

Gunnar's dark eyebrows snapped together, and he whipped his head toward his younger sister. "What?"

She shook her head smugly and rolled her eyes. "Come on, Gunnar. I may be sixteen, but I'm not naive. I know sexual tension when I see it, and you two are giving off so many pheromones that wild animals are going to start showing up here in a minute."

Gunnar frowned and shot Derek a look. "What have you been teaching her, Doc?"

Derek lifted both hands. "Don't look at me."

Then twitching a grin, he added, "And for the record, I agree with Piper. I'm also sensing a certain...*vibe* between you two."

Violet's mouth opened, but only a sort of choking sound came out. A sexual vibe between her and the boorish linebacker? No way...

Gunnar scoffed and backpedaled from their nose-to-nose standoff, grumbling, "Give me a break."

With one last dark glance at her, the older Colton brother stormed back toward the SUV.

"So then you're okay with them filming here as long as they avoid your cabin?" Derek called after him.

When Gunnar didn't answer, Derek grinned mischievously at Mac. "I think that's a yes. When do you want to start?"

Get a room? Gunnar gritted his back teeth as he stormed back to the Suburban. If Piper weren't too old to spank...

He huffed out a frustrated breath. Who was he kidding? He'd never lay a hand on his sister in the name of discipline. But that mouth of hers! And when had his baby sister learned about sex and pheromones, for cripes sake? The idea Piper had become a young woman while he was deployed unnerved him, and the thought of some randy teenage boy coming sniffing around his sister...

Gunnar flexed and balled his fists a few times to work out the tension. He knew all too well what boys Piper's age thought about girls. It was pretty much the same thing men his age thought about women—especially perky young women with short blond hair and Bambi eyes...sassy, petite women with ample curves and pouting lips that begged to be kissed...

Grunting, Gunnar scrubbed a hand over his face. Damn it, Piper was right. As annoyed as he was to see the film crew on the ranch property, Gunnar had found trading barbs with the feisty actress incredibly...invigorating, arousing.

Yanking open the driver's door of the ranch's Suburban, Gunnar growled under his breath. If he wanted to get involved with a woman—which at this juncture in his life, he did *not*—a spoiled and superficial starlet was the last person he'd consider for a fling. And a starlet with *kids?* He shuddered. No thank you. He was not a glutton for punishment.

Cranking the engine, Gunnar glared through the windshield at the people assembled on the ranch lawn, and a sour feeling gnawed his gut. He knew he'd been inordinately rude. Guilt kicked him for having assumed a hostile demeanor. But after the incident in town, his nerves were already jangling, and all he wanted was to go back to his cabin, reheat some leftover stew for dinner and kick back in his recliner for the Penn State football game—alone, without distractions. He wanted to think—or *not* think if his thoughts dwelled too long on the way he'd made a fool of himself in town or the fool of himself he'd made in front of the movie crew.

He squeezed the steering wheel impatiently as Violet Chastain's dressing room bus lumbered down the driveway, out of his path. He cut another glance to the tiny woman who'd stood up to him like a warrior or a mama bear when he'd challenged her. The spark that had lit her brown eyes had intrigued him, enticed him. He sent an appreciative gaze over her formfitting green minidress and tan leggings, the spots of color the cold air put in her cheeks. With her pixie haircut, petite stature and gamine face, was it any wonder she conjured images of Tinkerbell for him? She was a grown-up Tinkerbell...with a hot body and lush mouth. And a dead husband. And kids.

Gunnar shook his head to clear it and jammed the SUV in gear as the bus finally cleared the road. The blonde actress stirred too many confusing and contradictory feelings in him. His gut told him she was trouble with a capital *T*. While the movie crew filmed in town and at the Double C, he'd do well to stay far away from the temptation and aggravation that was Violet Chastain.

Violet stamped up the steps into her tour bus, then stopped for a moment as a shiver rolled through her from the cold, from unspent adrenaline after her confrontation with Gunnar, and from…okay, lust, because Gunnar Colton, jerk that he was, had a to-die-for physique, a rough-hewn square jaw and knee-melting hazel eyes. Too bad he had the personality of an angry badger.

The rest of the Colton family she'd liked. Derek had been charming and gracious. Piper was clearly bright, if starstruck, while Sawyer seemed shy and soulful, his dark eyes keenly assessing, much like her Mason's did.

As if her thoughts of her contemplative son had conjured him, Mason toddled out of the bus's bedroom and spotted her. "Mommy!"

"Hey, sunshine!" Violet hurried to scoop her son into her arms for a hug. "All done napping?"

Mason gave her wet kisses, then pressed his chubby hands to her face. "Cold."

"Yeah, it's cold outside. Brrr!" She poked her chilled nose against his cheek, which still bore the impression of his blanket from his nap, and he shrank back giggling.

"Brrr!"

"Mommy!" Hudson's voice preceded him as he came charging out of the bedroom with no diaper on.

Violet stooped to greet her second son, laughing. "Well, hello young streaker. Do you have a kiss for me?"

Hudson smacked a kiss on her face, then turned and darted away as his nanny appeared in the bedroom door.

"Hudson, you scamp! Get back here and put on some pants, mister!" Rani Ogitani propped a hand on her hip and shook her head. "I've never seen a kid with so much energy! And believe me, I've babysat for some rambunctious kids in my day."

"Rani, I bless the day I found you. I don't know what I would have done these past few months without your help with the kids."

The nanny grinned. "Oh, probably hired someone else just as competent."

"Not likely." After going through three nannies in eight months, Violet had mentioned her child care troubles to an old high school friend, with whom she kept in touch through email. Her friend, Zoe Bancroft, mentioned that her baby-sitter was looking for a job as a full-time nanny and gave Rani high marks. A week later, Rani had moved from Louisiana to Beverly Hills to live with Violet, Adam and the boys.

Violet shook her head. "No one's better than you, and the proof is in how my boys are thriving, even without—" a rush of emotion overwhelmed Violet, and her throat closed "—you know…Adam…"

Her nanny gave her a sympathetic smile. "They are thriving because of the love and attention you give them."

Or don't you Hollywood types believe in raising your own children? Gunnar Colton's accusations reverberated in her memory, and she sighed.

"I wish you would tell that to the linebacker," she mumbled, then wondered why she gave a fig what Gunnar Colton thought of her parenting skills. Perhaps because he prodded her working-mommy guilt over leaving so much of her children's care up to Rani.

"Linebacker?"

"Never mind." She stood and held Mason out to her. "Here, you take this one, and I'll round up the streaker and finish dressing him."

Rani held up a hand of refusal. "Wait." She turned her head and coughed several times into the crook of her arm. "Sorry. I'll take him now."

Violet frowned. "Are you coming down with something?"

"I hope not." Rani rested Mason on her hip and brushed his blond curls out of his eyes. "Maybe it's just the changing weather or dry air or something. I can't seem to shake this cough."

"I'll watch the boys for a while if you want to rest. I told the Yoders I'd be back for dinner, but if you need—"

"I'm okay. I grabbed a short nap while the boys were asleep. Besides, don't you need to go over the new script for the barn scene they sent over this morning?"

"New script? They changed the barn scene

again?" Violet's shoulders sagged. "I wish they'd make up their minds. I wanted to be through shooting by Christmas. The boys should be in their own home on Christmas morning."

Rani turned her head and covered another cough. "Mac still think that can happen?"

"It'll be close."

The hydraulic hiss of the bus door opening announced a new arrival, and Violet turned.

"Knock, knock," Mac called as he poked his head around the corner. "Everybody decent?"

"Everyone except Hudson," Violet said, meeting her director in the living area of the bus and scooping Hudson off the couch where he was bouncing on the cushions. She turned to ask Rani to grab a diaper out of the boys' bag and discovered, as usual, Rani was a step ahead of her. The nanny tossed her a diaper and a toddler-size pair of overalls. Violet caught the diaper. Mac snagged the overalls and eyed them.

"I didn't know they made these for tykes."

Violet had the diaper fastened around Hudson in a few deft motions, then took the denim clothes from her director. "They make just about anything you can imagine in babies' sizes. But I'm sure you're not here to discuss toddler fashions. What's up?"

"Just making sure you're all right. If you think that Gunnar fellow is going to be a problem, we can look for another location—"

"I'm fine. And this ranch is perfect for the scenes at the lawyer's house. I'm sure if we stay out of the big bad wolf's way, he'll stay out of ours."

"Bad woff!" Hudson repeated. "Puff, puff, bwooooow!"

Mac gave Hudson a raised eyebrow glance.

"I'll huff and puff and blow your house down," she said to clarify as she struggled to button Hudson's overalls while he hopped up and down on the couch. "*The Three Little Pigs* is one of the boys' favorite stories."

Her son filled his cheeks and acted out the scene from the fable while grinning impishly.

"Okay, I'll sign the contracts with Dr. Colton then. Did you get a chance to look over the revised script? I'd like to shoot the barn scene tomorrow."

Violet winced. "No, I haven't. How much did the script change?"

"A lot. We decided to combine a couple scenes. Jan now has Matthew showing up while Grace confronts Luther, and the three of them have it out."

Jan Teague, the lead writer for *Wrongfully Accused,* had won numerous awards for her past scripts, so Violet trusted her to do the right thing for the movie. But the constant last minute changes were exhausting to keep up with.

"I'll have to burn some midnight oil—literally—" because her Amish host family didn't have electricity and used oil lamps instead "—but I'll be ready in the morning."

Mac chucked her lightly on the chin. "That's my girl. Things okay at the Yoders?"

Benjamin and Alice Yoder, an Amish couple with three children in Paradise Ridge, had agreed to let Violet live with them for several weeks in order to immerse herself in her role as Amish woman Grace Moon. Violet wanted to understand and appreciate the nuances of the Amish lifestyle, religion and traditions in order to bring more authenticity to her character. She was learning a tremendous amount about the Amish community while staying with the Yoders, but in order not to crowd and add chaos to the Yoders' home, her boys and Rani were staying in the bed-and-breakfast rented by the film crew. She missed the time away from Mason and Hudson, but the arrangement was better than leaving them in California for several weeks while she shot the movie in Pennsylvania.

Mac pulled a frown. "I know the recent abductions and murders have the Amish community on edge."

"Not just the Amish community. I'm a little spooked myself, but…yes, things at the Yoders are fine," Violet said.

In recent weeks, three Amish girls had disappeared from the community, and two of the teenagers were later found dead in a remote cabin. The shock of the tragedy had sent rip-

ples through not just the Amish families of Paradise Ridge but the film crew as well—especiall
since the real life events bore some similarity t
the story line of the movie.

But Violet couldn't credit the recent crime
for the odd jitters dancing inside her. No, th
blame for her butterflies belonged to a certai
sexy boor with soul-piercing hazel eyes. Gur
nar Colton was far more dangerous to her peac
of mind.

Chapter 2

"Mary, I want you and your brothers to deliver this food before school," Alice Yoder said and placed a basket on the wooden table next to a burlap sack.

Violet looked up from her breakfast of fresh baked bread with honey, fried ham and scrambled eggs with homemade cheese. Her Amish family might not use many of the conveniences the modern world took for granted, but Alice Yoder's cooking was heavenly.

"*Ja, Mamm,*" seventeen-year-old Mary replied, then glanced toward Violet and said, "Yes, Mother."

Violet shook her head. "No, don't speak English for me. I want to learn Dutch."

Mary glanced at her mother, who gave a nod, and the teenager faced Violet again. "As you wish."

Alice finished instructing her daughter about the delivery in Pennsylvania Dutch, and the only words Violet understood were a name: Caleb Troyer.

"Troyer? Isn't he the man whose sister was kidnapped?" Violet asked, her gut pitching with empathy for the young Amish man.

Alice's face reflected her concern for Caleb. "*Ja*. His sister, Hannah. He's been working with the *Englischers* to find her, which doesn't leave much time for preparing meals. It is our duty to look after Caleb and his precious daughters during this difficult time."

Violet smiled. "I think it's awesome the way the Amish community rallies around their neighbors in times of crisis."

"Awesome?" Mary blinked and frowned.

Violet realized her slang use of the term must have confused the girl.

"Oh, by that, I mean that it's wonderful. Kind and generous."

Mary nodded and fingered the strings of her black *kapp,* the head covering worn in respect for God and signifying her unwed status. Because of her role as an unwed Amish woman, Violet also wore the traditional dress, apron and black *kapp* that she would wear as Grace during the filming.

"William, David, are you ready for school?" Alice called to her young sons.

The two boys ran in from outside, their cheeks ruddy from the cold, and Alice handed them their burlap bags. "Go with your sister, and take these to Caleb Troyer. Go now. Don't be late for school."

Violet shoved to her feet. "I'll walk with them. I'd like to meet Caleb and his family, offer my assistance, as well."

Alice handed Mary the basket and kissed her daughter's cheek. "You may walk with Mary and the boys, but do not be offended if Caleb refuses your offer. We take care of our own but do not want outside influences or help from *Englischers*."

"I understand." Violet pushed away from the table and hurried to the door to catch up with Mary and the Yoder boys. "Thank you for breakfast, Alice. I'll help you clean up when I get back."

Alice waved her out the door. "No, you are our guest. Go on before the boys leave you."

William and David had, in fact, already trotted to the road that led to the Yoder's farm. Mary lifted a hand to wave goodbye to her father, tending the horses in the stable, and Violet, pulling on a thick cape for warmth, hustled to catch up, her feet crunching through the thick frost. Her plain leather lace-up boots and calf-length skirt of her dress made running difficult, especially on the uneven earth of the Yoder's farm, but Mary lingered at the road, waiting for her.

"How far is the Troyer's home?" Violet asked,

readjusting her *kapp,* which had come askew as she rushed.

"Not far." Mary pointed down the rural road. "It is the next farm. Only two miles."

Violet chuckled, her breath forming a white cloud in the cold air. "Your definition of not far and mine are a little different. No wonder you all can eat so well and stay in shape."

Mary angled her a shy smile and started to ask a question but was distracted by her brothers' playful bumping and swatting of each other. "William, settle down."

"I can beat you to the next road!" David shouted and took off running. William cast a quick glance to his sister then gave chase.

"David!" Mary called to no avail. She sighed heavily. "Boys are so…" She waved a hand in frustration, clearly searching for the right word that wouldn't get her in trouble.

Violet caught the girl's hand in hers. "Yes, they are! Very…" And she raised her own hand in frustration, then laughed. Mary's smile broadened, and Violet clasped her other hand around

Mary's. "And they only get worse. Men are especially...aurgh!" Violet raised her eyes toward the sky in exasperation.

When Mary chuckled, Violet squeezed the teenager's hand and studied her lightly freckled face. Her fresh-scrubbed, makeup-free skin glowed with the dewiness of youth and innocence. Her wide gray eyes held no guile, only an earnest love for life, and her dark brown hair was twisted up in the traditional modest bun.

"Mary Yoder," Violet said, grinning, "do you have any idea how lovely you are?"

Her compliment obviously caught the girl off guard. A pink blush blossomed in her cheeks, and she ducked her head to hide a small smile before sobering a bit. She cast Violet a guarded look. "Vanity is a sin."

Ah, right. That belief was the reason why the Amish had no mirrors in their houses.

"Hmm, in that case I know quite a few women—and men—in Hollywood who are in big trouble!" Violet returned with a wink.

The rumble of a car engine drew Violet's attention to the large silver sedan that was driving rapidly toward them on the country road—far too rapidly considering how narrow the road was and how frequently the lane was used by Amish pedestrians or horse buggies, she thought, twisting her mouth in a scowl.

"Careful," she said, taking Mary by the arm to tug her farther from the road, "give this idiot—" Violet stopped abruptly as the silver car skidded to a stop a few yards ahead of them, blocking their path. Her immediate thought was the car had been sent by the production staff to find her. Was there an emergency with her boys? If that were the case, why hadn't they called her cell?

Violet patted her apron pocket—no phone. She'd left her cell on the bedside table at the Yoders'. Her pulse gave a little leap of concern, and she took a step toward the car.

The driver's and passenger's doors opened at the same time, and the two men who emerged wore ski masks. Alarm and confusion skittered through Violet, and even before she'd fully registered what was happening, she moved between the men and Mary. "What's going on?"

"We're going for a ride, sweetcheeks," one of the men chortled as they advanced on Violet and Mary.

Icy comprehension slammed Violet. Panic exploded in her chest. "Mary, run!"

Violet staggered backward, spun, grabbed Mary's sleeve as she scrambled to flee. But Mary was yanked from her grasp, and the girl screamed.

In the next second, a large hand seized Violet's cape and yanked her backward. She whirled, arms raised, ready for battle. Adrenaline flooded her, fueling her fight, and every self-defense lesson she'd learned flashed through her brain.

Eyes. Throat. Groin. Do not *let them take you to another location.*

As a beefy arm slid around her waist, hauling her toward the car, Violet slammed her elbow behind her as hard as she could, stomped the man's insole and reared her head back to smash his nose.

"Damn it, bitch! Stop that!" the man growled, digging his fingers in her arm.

She searched for Mary, fear for the Amish girl pounding through her.

"Fight them, Mary! Fight back!" she shouted as she struggled against her captor's grip. She thought of Hudson and Mason, and her chest tightened. She wanted to see her babies again, couldn't leave them orphaned. "Fight hard, Mary! Don't let them get you in the car—no matter what!"

"Shut up!" the man holding her snarled and smacked his hand across her cheek.

"You bastard! Let me go!" Violet clawed at the man's eyes. In her peripheral vision, Mary fell to the ground, and the other man snatched the girl's head back by the hair. Fury exploded in Violet. "Don't hurt her, you prick!"

"Such language," her captor mocked, seizing her around the waist and lifting her easily from the ground. "What would *Mamm* and *Datt* say if they heard you? You'd be shunned, for sure."

Violet aimed her boot heel at his kneecap and kicked. "I'm not Amish, jerk!"

Growling in pain, her captor loosened his grip and clutched at his leg. Violet struggled free and seized the opportunity. Gathering her wits and tossing off her encumbering cape, she assumed a combative stance.

"Nooo! Violet!" Mary wailed.

Violet jerked her gaze toward the teenager. The second man had Mary penned on the ground, his fist reared back.

"No!" Violet screamed.

The man's hand bashed Mary's jaw, and Violet flinched as if she'd received the blow.

"Not the face, idiot!" the other man shouted. "He said their faces can't be messed up!"

The next punch landed in the girl's gut. Mary cried out in pain, and, fury surging, Violet lunged at the man holding Mary. She threw herself on his back and wrapped an arm around his neck, squeezing, gouging at his face. "Get off her! Leave her alone!"

Immediately, Violet's attacker grabbed the

back of her dress and forcibly pried her off his partner. As she was dragged away, Violet struggled and fought the restraining arms. Twisting at the waist, she snagged her captor's ski mask and dragged it off.

A prickle ran through Violet when she realized what she'd done. His face! She had a chance to identify the kidnappers. Look at his face!

But a blow to the side of her head caught Violet off guard, and she reeled back, tripping and toppling dizzily to the ground. She had only a split second to brace herself before a booted foot collided with her ribs. All the air in her lungs whooshed out from the impact, and a throb of pain ricocheted all the way to her skull. Violet curled in a ball to protect her ribs, her belly. Tears puddled in her eyes.

Hudson and Mason…she had to survive this to see her boys again.

"Damn it, get the girl in the car! We gotta get out of here!"

The ski cap was snatched from her hand, and she groaned internally. Summoning every ounce of her strength, Violet blinked her vision clear, focused on gathering details while she had the chance. The pair of paint-splattered work boots inches from her head faced the other direction. Her captor had turned his back. She angled her gaze up, glimpsed his short brown hair, bleeding nose, snarling mouth. Then he yanked the ski mask back over his face and turned toward her.

"Can't leave no witnesses. I have to kill you now." When he reached under his jacket, terror spurred Violet to action. She rolled away from him, despite the ache in her side, and sprang back to her feet. She risked a glance toward Mary. The girl was sobbing, still thrashing, still fighting the man who was dragging her by the feet toward the open car door.

Violet's attacker advanced on her again, and a hunting knife flashed in his hand. Trembling, Violet backpedaled, scrambling mentally for a plan. She couldn't outrun the men. They outweighed her, outnumbered her, had Mary's life in their hands.

The knife-wielding thug edged closer. "Come on, bitch. You think you're so smart?"

Disarm him, her brain shouted.

When he stepped closer, Violet swung her leg up in a roundhouse kick, aiming for his wrist. But at that same moment, he stabbed at her in an arc, and the blade jabbed deep in Violet's thigh. Adrenaline masked the pain for the first several seconds, even when her assailant jerked the blade out and shoved her to the pavement. She landed with a bone-jarring, breath-stealing impact. The world around her blurred…slowed… muted.

Help! Help me, she screamed, but no sound came from her mouth.

Then white-hot pain seared her leg. She touched the wound and felt the sticky warmth of her own blood.

Straining to focus her eyes, she looked for her attacker and braced for another blow—the death blow.

"Get her arms!" The shout seemed to come

from the end of a tunnel…underwater…from a deep well.

Then she heard a scream—piercing, terrifying, chilling.

Violet searched for Mary. She saw the men lift her and shove her in the backseat.

Still Mary fought, wrenched one hand free and grabbed the car door.

Violet sucked in a ragged breath. *Mary!* She stretched an arm toward the sedan and dragged herself an inch at a time. Her leg throbbed, but she ignored the pain. Mary! She had to help Mary.

One of the brutes slammed a fist in Mary's gut, and the girl doubled over in pain. Her fingers slipped from the door. With a booted foot, the man shoved Mary inside and slammed the car door shut. "Go!"

Violet stretched out a trembling arm. "Noooo!"

With a squeal of tires, the silver sedan screeched away.

Horror punched Violet as she collapsed on the road, sobbing, "Mary!"

Chapter 3

Nausea roiled in Violet's gut. Her leg was on fire. Her head throbbed.

But the worst pain came from her heart. She felt flayed, raw. She was tormented by the knowledge that the kidnappers had taken Mary, had hurt Mary. God only knew what they had in store for the Amish girl.

Violet pressed a hand to the gash in her leg, curled in the fetal position and sobbed harder than she had since she was a child.

Mary! They had Mary!

Her head swam, and the road seemed to rock beneath her.

On some level, she knew she needed to get help. She was bleeding, losing consciousness and aching from head to toe.

But she couldn't erase from her mind's eye the look of terror on Mary's face as the animals shoved her in the backseat.

"Mary," she muttered, feeling her strength seeping from her.

The clop of horse hooves rattled through her skull, and a sudden shadow blocked the sun from her eyes.

"Mein Gott!" a male voice said.

Gentle hands rolled her onto her back, probed the wound on her leg and lifted her.

A vague image of a dark beard, black hat and grim mouth wavered before her. She moaned in protest as the man moved her. "Mary," she rasped.

The man said something to her in Pennsylvania Dutch as he laid her on a hard surface. The scents of dirt and horse sweat filled her nose, and she struggled not to retch. Near-blinding pain reverberated through her as the surface below her lurched into motion, bouncing roughly down the road. A buggy…

Violet's vision dimmed. Her consciousness faded in and out as her Amish rescuer jerked to a stop, shouted words she didn't understand. But a name filtered through the haze.

Troyer. She'd been on her way to visit Caleb Troyer. It was the next farm…not far.

"Mary…"

She heard more voices—urgent voices, young voices. "Violet! What happened?"

Hudson? Mason? No…David and William.

More German. Another name—Dr. Colton.

A bandage was wrapped quickly and tightly around her thigh. Dizzying pain shot through her. And then she was being lifted again.

This man was younger, strong, capable. Caleb Troyer?

"Hold on, Violet. I have you," he said in English, his voice compassionate and soothing. "We will get you to the doctor."

She tried to speak, had to tell them…what?

"Where's Mary?" one of the young voices asked. Mary...

Violet's mouth was dry, and her tongue felt swollen to twice its normal size. She tried to speak, tried to tell them. "Took...her..."

"Easy, ma'am. You are going to be all right. Dr. Colton is a good doctor. The best."

"Mary," she rasped, curling her fingers in the front of Caleb's shirt. "Took Mary..."

Caleb stilled, met her gaze with piercing gray eyes. "What?"

"They...took Mary..."

Pain filled Caleb's face, and his jaw tightened. She felt the tremor that shook him.

He set Violet down in another buggy and shouted something in Pennsylvania Dutch to the other man. As Caleb Troyer cracked a whip at his horses, sending the buggy forward with a lurch, he added, "And find Emma Colton. Tell her to meet me at her brother's office!"

Peering over the top of the résumé he held, Derek Colton studied the attractive blonde sitting across his office. "Your credentials are impressive, Ms. Phillips, but I don't see any references here."

Amelia Phillips's fingers tightened slightly on the arms of her chair. "Well, no. I didn't list any because—"

The door to Derek's office flew open. "Dr. Colton, come quickly!" his receptionist blurted without preamble. "We have an emergency."

Derek frowned as he lurched to his feet. "What is it?"

"An Amish woman. Caleb Troyer brought her in. She's bleeding badly and unresponsive." His receptionist jumped out of his way as he rushed to his office door.

His gaze flicked briefly to Amelia Phillips. "I'm sorry. We'll have to finish later."

Amelia nodded, her hazel eyes wide with concern. "Can I be of help?"

Derek hesitated, giving her a quick assessing glance. "I…yeah. Scrub in. Nancy will show you where everything is, then meet me in exam room two."

He turned without waiting for a response and hustled to the sink to wash his own hands and don a pair of latex gloves.

Caleb Troyer stood in the waiting room with a petite woman limp in his arms.

"Bring her back here, Caleb!" Derek shouted, motioning to the exam room where a vast array of top-notch medical equipment waited. When Derek had opened his practice in Eden Falls, Gunnar had quietly funded the purchase of state of the art facilities, setting Derek up to provide most any treatments or tests his patients needed.

Caleb hurried into the exam room and laid the woman gently on the exam table. "I don't know her name. Isaac Lapp found her on the road and brought her to my house. Her leg has a deep cut, and her head has a large bump. Bruises and scrapes…"

Derek stepped closer to begin his examination, and his breath froze in his chest when he saw the woman's pale face. "This is Violet Chastain, the actress! I just met her yesterday. Why would—"

Caleb caught Derek's arm in a firm grip, stopping him. "We need to get Emma here. The woman was still conscious when she arrived at my house. She said someone kidnapped Mary Yoder. I think the men who took my sister have Mary now, too."

Derek's pulse kicked, and he muttered a curse word under his breath as he began peeling the homemade bandage off Violet's leg. "Have my receptionist call Emma and Tate. You can wait out front for them, tell them what you know." He jerked a nod toward his patient. "Thank you for bringing her in."

As Caleb left, a scrubs-clad figure bustled in drying her hands on a sterile cloth. Derek arched an eyebrow. "That was quick."

"You have to be quick when lives are at stake, right?" Amelia peered past him to the exam table and snapped on a pair of gloves. Immediately, she clipped a pulse ox monitor on Violet's finger, then grabbed the blood pressure cuff from the countertop. "Heart rate 60. BP is 80 over 65. Oxygen 90 percent. Starting 2L oxygen now." She retrieved the oxygen tank and non-rebreather mask from the corner of the room and settled the mask over Violet's mouth and nose.

Derek cut Violet's skirt off her so he could work better, then opened his mouth to ask Amelia for a thigh cuff, only to find her turning from the cabinets with one in her hand. Amelia met his gaze. "Where do you keep your IV kits?"

He jerked his head toward the cabinet across the room. "Top shelf, left side. How are her pupils?"

"Even and responsive to light. Her skin is cool and clammy."

While Derek applied the thigh cuff, Amelia started a saline IV, finished undressing their patient, draped her with a sterile sheet and assessed Violet's other wounds.

Satisfied that Amelia knew what she was doing, Derek finished unwrapping the pressure bandage Caleb had tied around Violet's leg and frowned at the deep gash. "Looks like she was stabbed. There's separation through several layers of muscle and—"

Amelia dabbed the wound with a piece of sterile gauze, absorbing some of the pooling blood so that Derek could better examine the severity of the injury, then flushed the wound with saline. He flicked a startled glance to her as she ripped open a suture tray before continuing. "Thanks." He carefully probed the wound with a long swab. "The femoral artery appears to be intact, thank God, but several smaller veins will need ligation. What did you find?"

"Abrasions and contusions to her head and face but nothing critical."

"Okay, push fentanyl and midazolam. Let's get her sewn up."

For the next hour, Derek labored over Violet's laceration, ligating the torn blood vessels and suturing the layers of muscle and skin. While he worked, Amelia monitored the actress's vitals and cleaned the less serious scrapes and bumps. With gently probing fingers, she felt Violet's scalp and searched her hair for other wounds. "In addition to the bump on her forehead, she's got a rather large knot just over her right ear.

External swelling. Do you want to send her to the hospital for a CT scan?"

"No need. I have a machine here. I'll have my tech do a scan when I'm finished with her." With the crisis past, Derek paused and watched Amelia work for a few seconds, remembering how she'd anticipated his every need, known and executed protocol without his directives, and ably and efficiently assisted him on every aspect of Violet's treatment. "I appreciate your jumping in the mix and helping out. You were a model of professionalism and composure under pressure."

Amelia cut a quick awkward glance toward him as she wiped disinfectant on Violet's scraped cheek. "I'm glad I could help."

Derek bent his head over his suturing, pulling closed another small stitch. "You did more than help. Your nursing skills may have made the difference in saving Violet Chastain's life."

Amelia's head snapped up. "Violet Chastain?"

Derek pulled a grin. "The one and only…our patient."

Amelia's hazel eyes widened as she studied

her patient's face. "Holy cow, it is! I thought she was Amish…I mean, the dress and…"

Derek chuckled. "Violet's here filming a movie. She plays an Amish woman, which explains her clothing." He frowned as he snipped the surgical thread he'd just tied off. "Someone should call her director, let him know about Violet. I have his number in my desk."

Amelia nodded and chewed her lip. "If her laceration is a knife wound as you suspect…"

When she let her sentence trail off, Derek eyed her, puzzled by her obvious uneasiness. "The police are already on their way, if that's what you're asking. We have reason to suspect a girl Violet was with when she was attacked was kidnapped."

Amelia's eyes widened. "Oh, no! How horrible!"

"Exactly." He lowered his gaze to Violet's wound and began applying an antibiotic ointment and pressure dressing. "She'll need a tetanus booster before she leaves, but you can wake her up. I'm finished."

Derek removed his latex gloves and headed to the sink to wash up, cutting side glances to the nurse who'd performed so admirably under pressure. References or not, he wanted someone with her ability and cool head on his team. "Ms. Phillips?"

Amelia glanced at him.

"I think you've just been baptized by fire. If you want the job, it's yours."

A bright smile lit her face, and he was struck again by how attractive she was. "Thank you, Doctor. I accept."

"Ms. Chastain?"

Violet angled her head toward the door where an auburn-haired woman and tall, rugged-looking man with light brown hair waited.

"Yes?" she said weakly, her body and emotions both drained to empty.

"I'm FBI Special Agent Emma Colton, and this is my brother, Philadelphia detective Tate Colton. We're working the case involving the abduction of Amish girls in the area. If you feel up to it, we need to ask you some questions," the woman said.

Though she had no energy, a heavy heart and a painkiller-induced daze muddying her thoughts, Violet knew she had information the police needed to rescue Mary. "I'll do my best."

Emma Colton stepped in and moved the chair beside Violet's bed. Tate was propped against the wall, a mini-recorder in hand, ready to take her statement.

"Tell us what happened to you and Mary." Emma flipped open a notepad. "Start at the beginning, and don't leave anything out, no matter how minor the detail may seem."

Violet tried to shift into a position more conducive for the interview, but her weak arms gave out and her injured leg, elevated with several cushions, throbbed in protest. Sighing and sinking back into her pillow, Violet let her mind rewind to that morning, to Mary's sweet smile.

Vanity is a sin.

Violet's heart wrenched, and moisture puddled in her eyes. "I was…walking with Mary to Caleb

Troyer's farm. Taking him food." She wet her dry lips and squeezed the blanket covering her. "Mary's brothers had run ahead."

With effort, Violet related the whole terrifying incident from the moment the silver car had screeched to a stop in front of them, blocking their path, to the gut-wrenching moment the men shoved Mary into the backseat and raced away.

"You said you were able to pull one of the men's ski masks off." Emma met her gaze. "Did you see his face?"

Violet nodded. "Briefly. Just a glimpse."

"Could you describe him to a sketch artist to compose a rendering?" Tate asked.

Violet shifted her gaze Tate. "I'll do whatever I can to get Mary back." More tears flooded her sinuses and dripped from her eyelashes. "They hurt her. Hit her." She shook her head, and guilt stabbed her. "It's my fault."

Emma frowned. "What is your fault?"

"I told her to fight them. To resist. She did and…they hurt her."

Emma wrapped her fingers around Violet's

wrist. "Don't take this on yourself. The only ones to blame are the bastards who took her and the evil men behind this online sex ring."

Violet's heart lurched. "Sex ring?"

Emma and her brother exchanged dark glances, and Violet felt her gorge rise. She swallowed hard to keep from retching.

"The kidnapped girls are being solicited online for sex and other depravities," Tate said grimly.

Violet trembled, imagining innocent Mary Yoder in the hands of such sick men, forced into perverted situations and abused for the pleasure of vile men. "Dear God…Mary!" She divided a stricken, panicked glance between Emma and Tate. "You have to find her! She's just seventeen! She just a precious, innocent girl, who—"

"I know. I know." Emma squeezed Violet's fingers, interrupting her. "We're as appalled and disgusted by this case as you are. And we are doing everything we can to get these girls back. I promise you. The information you have could be key to recovering not only Mary but…" Emma paused, and through their joined hands, Violet felt the FBI agent shudder. "Caleb Troyer's sister was taken, as well."

A bone-deep fatigue and grief washed through Violet. She closed her eyes, searching for the strength to continue the interview. Mary's life, the lives and innocence of the other missing Amish girls lay in her hands, in her ability to remember and identify her attackers.

Can't leave no witnesses. I have to kill you now.

Icy fear settled over her like a cold morning fog. "They…they meant to kill me," she rasped.

"What?" Tate asked stepping closer to the bed, his brow furrowed.

"Because I saw his face. I can identify him and—" she shivered "—he said he had to kill me."

Emma and Tate exchanged worried looks.

"I think they believed I would die from my wounds…or they wouldn't have left me."

The monitor registering her heart rate began to beep loudly, and Derek Colton, followed by a blonde woman in scrubs, hustled into the recovery room. "Interview's over. Her heart rate is too high."

Emma scowled. "Derek, we still have questions about—"

"The interview is *over*," the doctor repeated firmly. "For now. My patient needs rest, not more stress."

"We need to arrange protection for her." Tate slid the mini-recorder in his shirt pocket. "If word leaks out that she survived the attack, the thugs who stabbed her will come after her."

Violet's stomach pitched. "Oh, God."

"We can post an officer at the door of your hospital room," Emma offered.

Violet raised a trembling hand to her temple and shot a pleading glance to Dr. Colton. "Please…can't I recover at home? Hospitals… there's no such thing as privacy for a public figure at a hospital. There'll always be another patient or dietary worker or orderly looking to make a fast buck selling info about the famous patient in room 323." In the case of her late husband, the leak had been a candy striper confiding to the wrong friends that she'd delivered flowers to *the* Adam Ryder, who was recovering from a drug overdose. Except Adam hadn't recovered and the media frenzy had been salt in an already bitter wound. Violet sighed. "News that I survived the attack is sure to get out if I go to the hospital."

"Do you really think the bed-and-breakfast where the movie crew is staying will be any more private?" Dr. Colton asked. "You need to be somewhere a medical professional can keep tabs on your progress or any setbacks."

Violet frowned, too tired to have to deal with major decisions but desperate not to be thrust into a volatile situation. "I can…hire a private nurse."

"Derek," Emma started, clicking her ball point pen closed and clipping it to her pad, "we have plenty of rooms at the ranch. With Tate and I both staying in the main house until this case is closed, she'll have protection. Plus you can check in on her anytime."

Derek arched an eyebrow, and Violet shook her

head. "I couldn't impose. Surely, there's some other—"

"The ranch is the perfect solution. Privacy, protection, someone there around the clock..."

"But—" Violet glanced from one Colton to another "—I..."

"Unless you have serious objections or a comparable, viable alternative..." Derek folded his arms over his chest and cocked his head, inviting her to state her case.

"I...I..." Violet's muddled and weary brain blanked.

"Then the ranch it is. Doctor's orders." Derek lifted the corner of his mouth in a Denzel Washington–worthy grin.

"And you're not an imposition. We're glad to have you," Tate said.

Violet's head spun, and she couldn't be sure if it was the painkiller or the speed of changing events. "My kids..."

"Bring them and their nanny. The nursery hasn't been used since Sawyer outgrew it. Your boys will love it." Derek headed for the door, aiming his finger at his siblings. "I'm going to take care of another patient now. No more questions for her until she's had a chance to sleep a few hours."

Tate scrubbed a hand over his face. "I'll go make arrangements to transfer her to the ranch. We'll need a way to distract the media long enough to get her in a vehicle without detection."

Violet's heart sunk. "The media is here? Already?"

"We had to notify your director, and word got out." Emma sat back in the chair and pulled a face that expressed her low opinion of the paparazzi. "Don't worry. We'll get rid of the vultures before you're moved. I promise we'll keep you and your family safe."

"Vampires." Casting a disgruntled glance to the gathering of reporters and photographers crowding the parking lot, Gunnar left the ranch's SUV at the back door to Derek's office and punched the keypad to the security system to let himself in his brother's clinic. He'd been having a late breakfast with Emma at the main house when his sister had been called in to Derek's clinic to follow up on a new development in the Amish kidnapping cases. Apparently another girl had been abducted, and the bloodthirsty media couldn't wait to broadcast the juicy details of the poor girl's misfortune. "No comment!" he shouted to the news crew that shoved a microphone in his face and tried to shoulder their way into the clinic. "Get lost or we'll arrest you for trespassing."

He yanked the door closed and stalked down the hall, grumbling under his breath. He found Derek in his office and folded his arms over his chest. "So…what's going on? Emma was all cryptic on the phone about needing the SUV and some muscle for a transport."

Derek rose from behind his desk. "That's right. First we have to send a decoy out, a goose for the paparazzi to follow, then we'll load Violet and her kids in the SUV for you to drive to the ranch."

Gunnar frowned. "Violet? As in Chastain? As in the starlet I met yesterday?"

"The same." Derek motioned for his brother to follow. "She's back here."

"Whoa. Hold up, Doc. Are you telling me you got me out here to play chauffeur for an actress?"

Derek faced him. "We need your help, and we needed the SUV. It's important that Violet not be followed. We have to protect her, assure her privacy."

"Why?" Gunnar grumbled. "That part of the contract you signed yesterday for them filming on the ranch? I asked to be left out of that, remember?"

Derek frowned and stepped closer, pitching his voice lower. "This has nothing to do with the movie. Violet is my patient. She was attacked today and nearly bled out. The girl she was with was kidnapped."

Gunnar stiffened, straightening his back and raising his chin. A prickle of guilt for his surly assumption slithered down his back. "Oh."

"Yeah, oh. Violet got her attacker's ski mask

off for a moment and saw his face. Emma fears the guy might come after Violet. Try to kill her to keep her quiet."

Gunnar drew his brow into a V. "Hell."

"Guess you saw the cameras outside?"

"Out in force." Gunnar rubbed his unshaven chin, an itch of suspicion starting between his shoulders. "So I'm part of some police operation to get Violet into hiding somewhere?"

"Exactly."

His fists clenched. He might be highly trained and capable of this bait and switch transfer, but the idea of putting his skills on the line left him unsettled. When he'd left the military, he'd thought his "operation" days were over. Helping execute Emma's plan was an uncomfortable reminder of his last mission in Afghanistan—and his greatest failure.

A high-pitched squeal rang down the hall, and Gunnar turned in time to see a blond-haired toddler race into the corridor giggling…and then a second, a carbon copy of the first.

A young woman of about college age appeared, her face pale and her eyes reflecting deep fatigue. "Come on, you rascals. Not today. Rani is too tired to play chase."

"Patients?" Gunnar asked Derek.

"No. They're Violet's twins and her nanny. Your passengers."

Gunnar's gut pitched. Being around kids was hard enough without being responsible for them, even if only for the few minutes it took to drive them to—

"And where am I taking them?"

Derek continued down the hall, waving Gunnar forward. "The ranch, of course."

Gunnar's steps faltered. "What?"

Derek stepped into a room where Emma and Tate conferred in one corner and a blonde nurse tended to the wisp of a woman laid up in a bed. Gunnar almost didn't recognize the injured woman as the same pixie who'd stood up to him yesterday. Violet Chastain's eyes looked hollow, sunken and desperately sad. Garish cuts and bruises marred her porcelain skin, and her cheeks, which had sported spots of color as they'd sparred yesterday, now had a sickly pallor. Propped with pillows, her leg was bandaged, her foot bare. The scrubs she wore hung loosely on her petite frame, making her appear even tinier and more defenseless.

Her doelike brown eyes met his as he stepped in the room, and instead of the crackle of attraction he'd experienced yesterday, Gunnar felt mule kicked. She held his gaze only long enough to register his presence, then turned away.

An image of the broken bodies that had littered the marketplace in Kabul flashed in his mind's eye, and his breath hung in his lungs. Violet Chastain's vulnerability raked through him, scraping raw memories. He shuddered, and fisting his hands at his sides, he crammed the haunting echoes of the bombing down, locked them away. In their place, a protective instinct and warrior spirit surged to the forefront. Some bastard had done this to her, had beaten her and kidnapped an innocent Amish girl. Fury poured through him until he shook with it. A mandate to defend her, to avenge her, to heal her blind-sided him.

"Oh, good, you're here," Emma said when she saw him. "So here's the plan. Derek's receptionist has volunteered to be our decoy. She'll be dressed up in some of Violet's clothes, sunglasses, hat, the works, and Tate will pretend to be escorting her back to the movie set. They'll leave, and with luck, the media horde will give chase, clearing the parking lot for us to sneak Violet and her kids through the back door and into the SUV. You take them all back to the ranch, making sure you aren't followed, and get them safely into the house. Simple as that. Got it?"

"Got it." His voice sounded rough and raw even to his own ears, and when Violet raised a gaunt look to him, he experienced another gut kick.

Tate turned to Derek. "We're ready. Can she be moved now?"

Derek shifted his attention to the blonde nurse. "How are her vitals, Amelia?" The nurse rattled off the information while Derek checked Violet's bandaged leg. "Okay. She's good to go. Gunnar, she'll need that wheelchair behind you."

"Decoy leaving now." Tate headed up front to escort the receptionist out the front door.

Gunnar retrieved the wheelchair and rolled it to the bed. While the nurse lifted Violet's injured leg, removing the pillows beneath it, Violet began gingerly scooting her healthy leg toward the edge of the bed.

"Wait," Gunnar said, then scooped her carefully into his arms and set her down in the wheelchair.

She hissed in pain, and he narrowed a concerned look on her. "Okay?"

Violet nodded. "It wasn't you. Any movement hurts my leg, but I'm all right now." She gripped his hand. "Will you make sure Rani and my kids get in the car safely?"

Her hand felt so small on his, and the plea in her expression burrowed deep inside him. Gunnar's mouth dried. "Of course."

The nurse took her position behind the wheelchair, ready to roll Violet out when the coast was clear, and Gunnar marched down the hall to prepare the nanny and two toddlers to leave.

The nanny—Rani, Violet had called her—looked up when he entered the exam room where they waited. Her eyes were bleary, and her cheeks were flushed. Gunnar frowned at her haggard appearance but assumed the nanny was simply upset over Violet's injuries. She had the twins occupied with a snack of graham crackers and juice but rallied when she spotted him.

"Time to go?" Rani asked, then covered a cough.

"Soon. Do you have car seats for the kids? We'll need to install them before we leave."

She nodded and pointed to the corner of the room where two safety seats, three suitcases and a large diaper bag waited…along with two pet carriers.

"She's bringing animals?" Gunnar groaned, visualizing whimpering little Chihuahuas or yipping Pomeranians.

Rani nodded. "Romeo and Sophie." She paused

to cough, then added, "They're part of the family. She doesn't go anywhere without them."

Biting the inside of his cheek to keep from commenting on Hollywood divas and their portable mutts, Gunnar stepped close to the nearest carrier and peeked inside. A fuzzy black-and-white cat blinked back at him, three black spots decorating his nose. Gunnar arched an eyebrow, not sure if cats were an improvement over snippy dogs or not.

Once Tate called to report they had the entourage of reporters following them across town, Emma checked the parking lot for stragglers, then gave the all clear. Derek helped Gunnar load the luggage and cats and buckle the safety seats in the SUV, while Emma assembled everyone at the back door. When Derek gave the signal, Gunnar hustled Rani and the twins, one boy in each arm, to the Suburban. Derek buckled one boy in while Rani tended to the second. Gunnar swept the parking lot with an encompassing glance, and Amelia wheeled Violet out.

"Gunnar, will you do the honors again? It'll

save time," Emma asked, hitching her head toward Violet.

He answered by stepping to the passenger door and silently lifting Violet into the front seat and fastening her seat belt for her. He caught the faint scent of flowers as he leaned across her, and he gritted his teeth when an inappropriate spark of attraction spun through him.

"Damn!" Emma snarled behind him, then thunked him on the back. "Hurry up! Get the door closed."

Gunnar jerked back and closed the passenger door before facing his sister. "What's wrong?"

"Across the street. The car parked by the tree." She gave her head a slight hitch toward the street, her face taut with frustration and disgust. "Telephoto lens."

Amelia raised her head to look where Emma indicated, and she drew a sharp breath. Ducking her chin again, the nurse kept her head down and hurried back inside the clinic with the wheelchair as if she were the celebrity needing to stay out of sight.

Gunnar scowled at Emma. "Make sure the car doesn't follow me." Then to Derek, he said, "Let's move."

Chapter 4

Derek piled in the far backseat with Rani, and Emma took the middle seat with the twins while Gunnar drove. He kept an eye on his side and rearview mirrors, and while he didn't see any vehicle following them, he drove a circuitous route back to the ranch.

No one breathed easily until the Suburban was inside the gates of the Double C and hidden by the trees surrounding the property. Gunnar parked in front of the main house, and the loading process was reversed, except that he carried Violet all the way into the living room. He settled Violet on the long couch and helped her prop up her leg.

Piper and Sawyer appeared from the kitchen and gaped at their famous guest.

"Oh, my God! Ms. Chastain, are you all right?" Piper rushed to the couch and hovered at the end by Violet's feet. "Can I get you anything?"

Violet shook her head wearily and sank back on the sofa.

Without being asked, Gunnar moved a decorative pillow under Violet's leg and another behind her back. Derek and Emma, each toting a cat carrier, entered the room with the nanny and Violet's boys. The cats were released to sniff their new environment.

When Rani coughed again, a deep barking sound, Derek frowned at her and touched her forehead. "You sound terrible. How long have you had this cough?"

"A couple days," Rani answered.

When Emma moved up to crouch beside Violet and discuss how she thought the arrangements would work, Gunnar stepped back ready to ease out of the room and escape to his cabin.

Derek was checking Rani's throat and feeling her forehead for a fever. The twins had been turned loose to run amok. To get away from the toddlers' groping hands, the black-and-white cat jumped up on a table, knocking over several framed photos in the process. The solid black cat scurried under a chair to hide. Sawyer, clearly hoping to distract the toddlers from his video game cases, turned the television to a cartoon channel. Piper continued hovering. Someone's cell phone rang. A toddler tripped and started crying. And up and up the noise level went. Up and up went the activity, tension level and confusion.

Yeah. Good plan, bringing a seriously injured woman to the ranch to recoup, Gunnar thought sarcastically. But since they hadn't asked his opinion, he kept his mouth shut and edged farther toward the exit…toward his nice, quiet, remote cabin…

"Gunnar?" Derek's voice reached him just as

he was turning the kitchen doorknob. He sighed and faced the living room. Derek crossed the floor, his expression grave. Crap. What now?

"The nanny is sick. She's got what is probably the flu, though I haven't had a chance to run a test yet. The kids can't be exposed to her, so I'm isolating her in the north wing."

"And you're telling me this because...?"

"Someone else will need to watch the boys."

"Why can't Julia do it?" he asked, referring to Piper and Sawyer's part-time nanny.

"Hopefully Julia can help babysit the twins in the evening, but during the day while Julia is at her other job..." Derek hesitated, his expression saying he knew he was asking a huge favor.

Gunnar tensed and aimed a finger at his brother. "Derek, do *not* finish that sentence. I beg of you."

"I work during the day, and I'm on call at night. Emma and Tate are on a case. Piper and Sawyer have school. You're the only one who—"

"I'll pay to bring in another babysitter or... or send them to day care somewhere. But don't ask me to take care of little kids." He held up a hand in protest, as if he could ward off what he knew was coming. "I don't know anything about babies!"

"Gunnar, it's only for a little while. Violet's too weak to take care of active toddlers. She needs to rest."

Gunnar looked past his brother into the bedlam of the living room. "Like she'll get any rest in that chaos."

Derek frowned and turned to survey the noisy, busy room. "You're right. This won't work. Violet needs sleep. And with her nanny sick, there's no one to keep tabs on her during the day."

Gunnar unwound a little. Finally Derek was seeing reason. "So she should stay somewhere else. Not at the ranch."

Derek gave a sharp whistle and waved Tate and Emma over. When they'd joined the huddle, Derek explained the situation to them. "I suggest we move her to Gunnar's cabin."

Gunnar choked. "What?"

"Good idea," Tate said, nodding, "She can

have the quiet she needs in the evening, and you can keep an eye on her and the kids during the day."

"And you're trained to protect her, should the need arise," Emma added.

"But—"

"I'll still stop in to monitor her progress, but I agree that your cabin is the best place for her."

"I don't!" Gunnar scowled at his siblings. "What's wrong with a private hospital or hiring a nurse to look after her and the kids?"

"What's wrong with you helping an injured woman in need of protection?" Tate's expression challenged Gunnar.

Emma shook her head with disappointment. "What's wrong with you, Gunnar? It's not like we're asking you to adopt her kids. Just keep an eye on them for a few hours during the weekdays. Piper can help on the weekends."

Three pairs of demanding eyes pinned him with expectant stares.

Gunnar felt a cool sweat break out on his forehead. His brain scrambled for a legitimate reason not to agree to his sibling's plan, while guilt and compassion for the waiflike woman on the sofa drummed his heart. "I…I don't…"

When he didn't finish his sentence, Derek nodded once. "All right then. Let's move her to Gunnar's cabin. The twins can stay here for now with Piper, but let's take the cats with us."

Gunnar raked both hands through his hair and heaved a sigh. Not only was the sassy pixie moving in with him, invading his private and tranquil retreat, but she was bringing her cats.

Violet stared up at the natural timber ceiling of Gunnar Colton's cabin and listened to the low rumble of voices from the next room. She fought her heavy eyelids, her fatigue the result of both blood loss and the powerful painkiller Dr. Colton had given her. If the Colton clan was going to make decisions that affected her, she wanted to be part of the conversation. But so far, because of her weakened condition, she'd been told who and what and when and where, and she'd feebly gone along with what Special Agent Colton and

Dr. Colton—Emma and Derek, they'd said she could call them—had decided for her.

Sophie, her black cat, hopped onto the bed and climbed onto her chest, where she head-butted Violet's hand, demanding attention. Violet nudged her off her bruised and aching chest, then scratched the feline behind the ear. "Hey, Sophie girl. Crazy day, huh?"

She heard the front door open and click shut, followed by heavy footsteps. Soon Gunnar appeared in the door of the spare room she'd been assigned, his large frame filling the portal. Though she'd been drifting in and out of sleep since receiving the painkiller for her leg, she'd been fully aware of Gunnar's muscular arms and broad chest each time he lifted her, moving her from one place to another as if she weighed no more than a rag doll. The blinds in her room were drawn, but enough sunlight seeped around the edges and through cracks that she could make out every hard line in his rough-hewn face. He wasn't smiling, though the day's events gave neither of them reason to smile.

"Do you need anything?" he asked.

Sophie eyed him warily, and Violet stroked her cat's head to calm the travel-stressed kitty. "Do you have any news about Mary Yoder?"

"That the girl who was abducted?"

Violet nodded. Her heart sat like a rock in her chest, full of fear for the girl, loaded with guilt that she'd survived the attack and not been taken, and aching with grief for the loving family who had to be missing Mary terribly tonight.

"No. But Emma said she'd be by later tonight to talk to you again. You can ask her then." He propped his shoulder on the door frame, crossing his arms over his chest. "So here's where we are. I've got instructions from Derek to make sure you stay in bed and rest, see to it you eat three squares a day, take your meds on schedule and watch your wound for new bleeding. Apparently tomorrow morning Emma will be dropping off your kids for me to babysit until Piper and Sawyer get home from school and their nanny arrives to supervise overnight at the main house." His frown deepened. "For the record, I have absolutely no experience with little kids. I'll keep them from sticking a fork in the electric outlet and make sure they don't sit around in messy diapers, but don't expect me to be all Mother Goose with them. I didn't sign up for this. I was drafted from a short list after my brother diagnosed your nanny with the flu and sent her to quarantine."

Violet closed her eyes with a resigned sigh. "I was afraid she was worse than she let on."

Gunnar was silent for a minute, and when she opened her eyes, he was staring at her with a wrinkle of consternation in his brow. Finally he pushed away from the wall and squared his shoulders. "Anyway…that's the sitrep. Any questions?"

"Sitrep?"

"Military shorthand. Situation report. Where things stand."

"Oh." Violet sank her fingers into Sophie's fur, drawing comfort from the presence of her pet in these strange and awkward circumstances.

"So…questions?"

She was too tired to think, to sort out everything that had happened today. "No."

He jerked a tight nod. "If you need anything, I'm in the next room." He turned to leave, and his tense manner reminded her of their first meeting. Had it only been yesterday?

"Gunnar?"

He stopped, his back visibly stiffening before he faced her. "Yes?"

"Why didn't you refuse? I can't believe there was no other possible arrangement for me and my children. I have resources…health insurance, money to hire a private nurse…"

He stared at her for a moment, his hazel eyes penetrating with their intensity. "The majority consensus was that this arrangement was best for you. To protect your privacy, to keep you safe and to allow you the quiet and calm you needed to recover."

"May I assume your vote was not part of that majority?"

He shrugged. "Whatever."

"You don't want me here."

"I didn't say that."

"You don't have to. It's pretty clear I'm an inconvenience. And my kids—"

"Look," he interrupted and stepped closer to the bed, "I didn't like the plan when Derek proposed it, no. But I'm not an ass, either."

Violet considered reminding him that his behavior yesterday suggested otherwise but kept the commentary to herself, considering she was dependent for the time being on his good graces.

"I'm not going to kick an injured woman and her children to the curb when they need help, even if that means I'm inconvenienced for a while. Derek and Emma are right. You're safest here. This is the quietest place on the ranch, where you'll also have someone around 24/7 to keep an eye on you. Derek says hiring outside help jeopardizes your privacy."

She narrowed her gaze on him. "And what about your privacy? Yesterday, you were pretty worried about the film crew bothering you in your refuge."

"Yeah, well, so I give up my privacy for a few

days. Small price for the greater good, huh?" But his tone said that his sacrifice still chafed.

Violet studied his strong jaw and rumpled dark hair. She'd wager the creases bracketing his mouth and eyes were the result of hard living, not laughter. Still, even with his grim expression, he was a strikingly handsome man. His impressive size and obvious physical strength filled her with a welcome sense of security. The sights and sounds of her attack were all too fresh in her mind, replaying in snatches like fast cuts from a movie. She suppressed a shudder and met his eyes. "Just the same...I appreciate your... cooperation. Your willingness to allow me—"

"Stop it." The furrow in his forehead deepened, and his mouth pressed in a hard line.

She blinked her surprise. "Excuse me?"

He scrubbed a hand over his face. "Don't thank me."

"Why not?"

"I'm not doing this for your gratitude or to curry favor with the 'big movie star.'" He drew quotation marks with his fingers, and his sarcastic tone spoke for his disdain.

Violet wilted into the pillow, rolling her head to the side and averting her gaze. "Forget it. I'm too tired, too emotionally wrung out to butt heads with you. Just let me sleep, okay?"

He said nothing for a while, then huffed a sigh and grumbled a curse word under his breath. "Sorry. That was a crappy thing for me to say."

She turned her head toward him again and forced her weary eyes to stay open. "Yeah. It was." He quirked an eyebrow, clearly surprised by her agreement, but she had always spoken her mind, even when her opinion wasn't popular. "What's more, it kinda negates your previous assertion that you aren't an ass."

His eyes widened, and he opened his mouth but made only a strangled sound of dismay. He stared at her, looking as guilty and chastened as a little boy caught kicking a puppy.

The corner of her mouth twitched in amusement. Apparently, she'd rendered him speechless, something she felt sure didn't happen often.

Gunnar rubbed his chin and narrowed a pensive gaze on her. "Granted, we got off on the wrong foot yesterday. But you can't judge me on—"

"*I* can't judge *you?*" she said with a startled laugh that made her ribs hurt. She winced and held her side, then returned her attention to him. "You've judged me based on your narrow, negative stereotype of Hollywood actresses, but you know nothing about the real me."

He braced his hands on his hips and gave her measured scrutiny. Twisting his mouth in thought, he nodded. "Touché, Tinkerbell. So what do you say we start over? Clean slate."

She smiled tiredly. "Works for me." Her eyelids drooped again, and this time she didn't fight the pull of sleep. "And now, I'm pretty worn out. I'd like to sleep before Emma comes by."

"Good idea." She heard the thud of his feet on the hardwood floor, but his steps halted too soon for him to have left the room. She sensed his gaze, studying her, staring at her. She knew she had to look pretty terrible after being roughed up: no makeup, her hair pillow rumpled—but she couldn't muster the energy to care. If he wanted to know the real Violet, this was who she was at the moment—ragged, worried, heartbroken…but determined to help the police bring Mary Yoder back home.

Gunnar took a beer from the refrigerator and twisted off the cap. He drank a swig of the cold brew as he walked into his living room and sank down on the leather couch. Lifting the remote, he turned his TV on to ESPN but left the volume muted in deference to Violet's need for sleep. Considering that the broadcast at this hour featured two analysts debating hot sports topics, watching the program without sound proved kind of pointless.

But Gunnar's mind wasn't on the BCS standings or the trouble a certain NBA star had gotten into. His mind was absorbed by the image of Violet laid up in his guest bed, her bruises standing out against her pale skin and her doelike eyes flashing with indignation at his thoughtless "big movie star" comment. Even after the hell she'd been through that morning, the woman had the pluck to put him in his place. The smile she'd given him after their truce had shot straight to his core, firing his protective instincts, his libido and his compassion at the same time. He couldn't remember another woman ever having such a potent effect on him.

When he recalled how small and vulnerable she'd looked when he first saw her at Derek's office, his gut wrenched. He was now responsible for her throughout the course of her recovery. He didn't take anything about that duty lightly.

He set his beer aside and leaned his head back on the sofa to stare at the natural-wood beams of his ceiling while pondering his uncharacteristic reaction to Violet Chastain. At some point, he closed his eyes and drifted off, because the next thing he knew, an odd noise was rousing him from a light sleep. Gunnar raised his head and rubbed his neck, which had gotten stiff as he slept. Darkness had fallen outside, and his stomach rumbled, telling him it was dinnertime. He was considering his food choices, knowing he had to fix something for Violet as well, when he heard the noise again—a cross between a puppy whimpering and woman's pleasured moan during sex. The sound came from the guest room where Violet was sleeping.

Gunnar sat forward, perched on the edge of the couch, and listened. The whining grew to more of a frightened whimper, and he swiped a hand over his face, debating his options. Did he charge in there and comfort her, as if he were a mother coddling a child or should he give her space and let her—

A loud thump and a sharp cry settled the matter for him.

Chapter 5

Adrenaline spiking, Gunnar lurched off the sofa and rushed into the dark room.

"Violet?" He heard the note of panic in his voice, a concern that ratcheted up a notch when he discovered she wasn't in the bed. A muffled sob reached him from the far side of the bed. He rounded the queen-size mattress, clicked on the bedside lamp and found Violet huddled in a ball on the floor, her feet tangled in the sheet that trailed off the bed.

"What the…?" Gunnar dropped to his haunches beside her and touched her tentatively on the back. "Violet?" Had the crazy woman tried to get out of bed and fallen?

A shudder shook her body, and she angled a teary-eyed look over her shoulder. "I was fighting…the men, and…I fell out of bed. I—"

Gunnar tensed and swept a searching glance around the room. "What men? Were they here?" Damn it, had someone broken in his cabin while he was asleep?

She shook her head. "Nightmare. I was reliving…" Her face crumpled, and tears spilled from her eyelashes. "It was terrifying. I've never been so scared."

He gritted his back teeth and swallowed a groan. Women's tears terrified him. What the hell was he supposed to do?

"Um, hey, let's get you back in bed. Okay?" He slipped his arm around her back and hooked the other under her legs. "Did you hurt yourself when you fell?" He picked her up from the floor and carefully settled her back on the bed, propping up the injured leg again on an extra cushion.

"It hurt, but I don't think..." She sighed and sniffled again. "I don't know. I just..." Violet wiped her face with her fingers and rolled her head back into her pillow. "I keep seeing Mary's face. The pleading look she gave me when they shoved her in the car...begging me to help her." Her voice cracked, and her wet brown eyes lifted to his. "I tried to reach her but I...I couldn't. I..."

Gunnar's stomach tightened, and he averted his gaze, focusing his attention on her bandaged leg. He didn't see any fresh blood that might indicate she'd pulled a stitch, but he made a mental note to call Derek and have him check on Violet later tonight.

"God only knows what those creeps are doing to that poor girl," Violet mumbled under her breath, her expression stricken, anxious.

Gunnar didn't tell her he had a pretty good idea what the girl was enduring, based on what he knew through Emma and Tate about the previous kidnappings. Rather than answer her, he worked on untwisting the sheet that was tangled around her ankle. "I was just about to make some dinner. Are you hungry?"

She shook her head.

"Come on now. I promised Derek I'd see that you ate something. You need to build your strength."

She stared up at him with hollow, haunted eyes. "Do you think they're feeding her?"

A fist closed around Gunnar's heart, a sympathy and connection to Violet that he didn't want to acknowledge. Trying to ignore the tightness in his chest and what he hoped had been a rhetorical question, he smoothed the sheet out and pulled it and the blanket over her. "I think I have some homemade vegetable soup in the freezer that Derek's housekeeper made and sent over last week. Sound good?"

Violet curled her fingers around his hand as he moved away, stopping him. "Will you stay here, just for another minute or two, until…"

He felt the tremble in her grip as another shudder rolled through her, and his gut pitched. He hadn't wanted to be drawn into the drama and tragedy of Violet's situation. He had his own baggage and nightmares to deal with, thank you very much. But looking into her eyes, seeing the dark shadows lurking in her expression, he saw himself. He saw the uncertainty and ghosts that stared back from his mirror. They'd both survived a trauma, witnessed a tragedy. And lived with the guilt and pain of all the "what ifs." What if he'd seen the suicide bomber sooner? What if the kidnappers had taken Violet instead of the Amish girl?

When he squeezed her fingers and sat on the edge of her bed, she clutched his hand between hers and twitched a tear-filled smile. "Thank you."

"Look, maybe…" He sighed and searched for something comforting to say. "Maybe you survived the attack so that you could help the police find Mary and the other girls who were taken. Maybe this happened so that you can help catch the people who did this."

"Yeah. Maybe." She looked and sounded unconvinced. "But I'd trade places with Mary in a heartbeat."

"Really? What about your kids? Where would they be if something happened to you?"

Her brow furrowed in consternation. "I don't know. Of course I'd never want Mason and Hudson to lose me after losing Adam. But Mary… she's so young and innocent. Being Amish, she's led a sheltered life. She has to be terrified." Her voice broke again, and new tears welled in her eyes.

Violet's concentration on Mary surprised him a little. Maybe she wasn't the self-centered and superficial starlet he'd presumed.

You know nothing about the real me.

Violet was right. He knew nothing about who she was and what she wanted from life. But he knew a little bit about where she'd been today and how she could get mired in the muck of her trauma. Unfortunately, he was still figuring out how to crawl out of that quicksand and not let it suck him under.

For her sake, though, he searched for a way

to give her hope and fire her will to fight back. "So here's what you do, okay?"

Her eyebrows dipped over her dark eyes, reflecting her skepticism, but her gaze held his as she listened.

"You follow Derek's instructions for getting better, and you work with Emma and Tate to bring Mary home and to help bring the bastards who took Mary to justice. Okay?"

As she nodded, a spark lit Violet's gaze, a resolve filled her expression with determination and hope. The fire reflected in her eyes burrowed into Gunnar and warmed him from the inside out. Without thinking about the gesture, he stroked her cheek with his free hand, drying the tears that had leaked from her eyelashes. She turned her face, leaning into his touch, and the intimate contact sent a shock wave rippling through him. He gritted his back teeth to rein in the kick of desire that pulsed through him. *Wrong time and circumstance, buddy.*

Violet's fingers tightened on his hand, and her gaze softened. "I like this side of you. Can you be *this* Gunnar—gentle and kind—when you're watching my boys tomorrow?"

He pulled his hand back from her cheek, self-conscious over his reaction to her. To cover his awkwardness, he flashed a lopsided grin. "What makes you think it's just a side of me and not the essence of who I am?"

Her eyebrows lifted. "Seriously? I've met grumpy Gunnar the jerk, remember?"

He pulled a face and shook his head. "Never happened. We started with a clean slate, right? Which means, as far as you're concerned, nice guy Gunnar is all you know."

She rewarded him with a half smile that made his pulse do a stutter step. "How convenient for you." Then, wrinkling her brow, she added, "But by that same reasoning, the only Violet you know is weepy, pitiful Violet who can't shake the horrid images of what happened today. Not such a good first impression."

Gunnar shrugged. "You say weepy and piti-ful. I say caring and sensitive. A bit traumatized but tough enough to pull through and be stronger for it."

She cocked her head, regarding him with a bemused expression. "Wow. How un-asslike. Nice Gunnar is really sweet, too."

He snorted his disagreement, and growing increasingly uncomfortable with the touchy-feely tone of the conversation, he disengaged his hand from hers.

"Yeah, my army buddies used to always tell me what a teddy bear I was," he said with a scoff.

She sighed and rolled her eyes. "And the grump returns…"

Gunnar opened his mouth to defend himself, but the words caught in his throat. Truth was, since returning from Afghanistan, he had been grumpy. He'd been restless and edgy and borderline depressed. Even he didn't like the Gunnar he'd become, so why should she?

He shoved to his feet and raked fingers through his hair. "So…is soup okay? I know I'm starved.

Maybe I'll open a can of those ready-to-bake biscuits to go with it. Hmm?"

She nestled down in the covers and closed her eyes. "No, thanks. I'm really not hung—"

"Hey!" he interrupted, his tone quiet but scolding.

Her eyes popped open, and she met his gaze with concern and query darkening her eyes. "What?"

He aimed a finger at her. "You promised to follow Derek's orders."

"I know, but—"

"No buts. You need to eat. If I have to, I'll spoon it in myself." He softened the ultimatum by keeping his expression light and teasing.

She blinked and tilted her head to the side. "Is that a threat?"

"Call it what you want, Tinkerbell." He strolled to the door, where he paused and gave her a smug grin. "But I was drafted to take care of you and get you back on your feet, and that's what's going to happen. I don't do things halfway, and I don't let my team phone it in, either. Got it?"

She gaped at him, her cheek twitching in amusement.

"Good. I'll be right back with your soup."

As Gunnar headed into the kitchen, a grin tugged his lips. For the first time in months, a sense of purpose fueled him and gave him direction. He was once again a man with a mission, and his mission's name was Violet Chastain.

Pop. The can of biscuits burst open, and Gunnar peeled the ready-to-bake dough off and set the pieces on the baking sheet for his toaster oven. Next he dumped the frozen block of vegetable soup into a microwave-safe bowl and started thawing it. As he worked, his mind tackled the problem at hand.

You know nothing about the real me.

He didn't like the fact that his disinterest in Hollywood gossip put him at a disadvantage concerning Violet. The whole world, it seemed, knew more about Violet than he did—even Piper, who, for all her proven genius, only bothered to learn about the things that interested her.

Fortunately, along with the typical teenage trifecta of boys, gossip and clothes, Piper showed an interest in all of the sciences, with a particular proclivity for computers.

Gunnar paused in the act of tossing out the biscuit can. Computers…

He darted a guilty glance at the guest room door, then took a seat behind the computer he had set up in his living room. He typed Violet's name in the search engine and hit Return, telling himself he wasn't gathering any information that wasn't widely held public knowledge. He was merely playing catch-up, not sneaking a peek at her private diary. Still, his conscience prodded him even as he opened the first web page.

The top result was a national news story published earlier that day:

Reports that Violet Chastain was injured on the set of her new movie, Wrongfully Accused, *were denied by the production company, but unconfirmed reports from sources close to the actress indicate Ms. Chastain was taken to a local doctor's office with life-threatening injuries.*

Sources close to the actress. Gunnar gritted his teeth in disgust, remembering their efforts to get her away from the paparazzi. How would it feel to know despite all your efforts to protect your privacy that the people closest to you couldn't be trusted not to sell your secrets, the most intimate details of your life?

He closed that page and surfed to the next link—a picture of Violet posing on the red carpet at the last Academy Awards ceremony and looking stunning in high heels and a form-fitting blue gown that emphasized her cleavage and had a slit that showed off her legs. Gunnar arched an eyebrow and studied the picture with interest. He wasn't surprised to see Violet looking so glamorous and sexy. She was a starlet after all, with a team of hairdressers and makeup artists and stylists to primp her to perfection. And he had seen her yesterday, looking good enough to eat in her green minidress and boots...

But somehow, seeing her all coiffed and polished like this seemed odd. The image on the screen reminded Gunnar of Audrey Hepburn, while the woman in his guest room reminded him of…well, Cat in the final scene from *Breakfast at Tiffany's*—wet, scared and heartbreakingly vulnerable.

Gunnar closed that web page and moved on to the next article, a report on Adam Ryder's death. A professional head shot of Adam Ryder accompanied the article, and Gunnar studied the smirking grin and classically handsome face of the Hollywood bad boy with the same regret he felt whenever he heard of someone dying too young—so much wasted potential.

My husband is dead, *you oaf!*

Shoving aside the memory of Violet's indignation with him, he scrolled down to read.

Adam Ryder, 28, husband of actress Violet Chastain and star of numerous box office hits including last year's Battlefield America, *died today at a Los Angeles hospital from an apparent drug overdose. An unidentified hospital employee reported that Chastain was at his side at the time of his death.*

An unidentified hospital employee, he read

again, and acid bit his stomach for the unethical breach of the family's privacy. With an angry click of his mouse, he closed that article and moved on. He continued to scan articles about Violet's charity work at a children's hospital, her trip to Iraq five years ago to entertain the troops and her movie and television credits, which spanned the past ten years. Gunnar grinned to himself as he clicked a link to a You-Tube clip of Violet in her first movie role at age sixteen. The walk-on part had her decked out as a goth teen, complete with black lipstick, spiked black hair and tattoos. Violet delivered her lines with all the sarcastic flippancy you'd expect of a teenage rebel before being pulverized by an alien death beam.

Noticing other Violet Chastain clips in the sidebar, he clicked the link for *The Journey Home,* the movie for which she'd been nominated last year for a best supporting actress Oscar. The scene had Violet standing in a living room with an older actor. Gunnar recognized the older man but couldn't remember his name. The actor was seated in a recliner and was hooked up to oxygen via a plastic tube. He and Violet had a tense exchange about her inheritance and his legacy and how all she'd wanted from the man was an apology but that the time for forgiveness had passed. Though the clip meant little to him out of context from the rest of the movie, Violet's facial expressions and body language were subtle and emotionally compelling, and her lines were powerfully presented. He played the clip a second time, focusing on the details of the scene from the lighting to the camera angles to the props. Violet had come a long way since her days as a victim of alien violence.

He clicked another link, titled "The scene that made me a fan of Violet Chastain." The scene began, and the image that appeared on his screen made Gunnar rock back in his chair in surprise. Violet and some Hollywood hottie du jour were naked and getting busy in a steamy shower. Like most movie love scenes, shot to stay within the R-rating parameters, while plenty of bare skin was visible, primarily his back, her legs and just a hint of her breast, the couple's tight embrace and strategically placed props kept the audience from seeing too much. Gunnar folded his arms over his chest and watched the scene with a scowl on his face and a restless urge crawling through him to peel the pretty boy off her by the scruff of his neck.

The scene progressed, and the lovers moved from the shower to the bed, hottie du jour carrying Violet chest to chest with her legs wrapped around his waist so that the audience got a brief look at her beautiful tush. Gunnar tightened his fingers into a fist and held his breath as the on-screen lovers writhed and kissed. When a noise startled the pair, loverboy levered away from Violet, and before the camera panned away, Gunnar and all of movie-going America was treated to a unhindered view of Violet Chastain's perfect breasts and peaked nipples.

Heat flooded Gunnar's veins, and his pulse thundered like the rapid fire of a machine gun. His body hummed with pure male lust, and his finger itched to rewind the clip for another glimpse of Violet's wares. But he didn't. He didn't need to. The image of naked Violet was burned into his brain. For several seconds, he simply stared at the frozen image where the clip had ended, his mind reeling, his body reacting the way any healthy man's would.

Realizing he was holding his breath, he exhaled a cleansing breath and sucked in a fresh lungful…that smelled of smoke. Smoke?

Clicking off the internet, Gunnar shoved his chair back and rushed into the kitchen where wisps of gray smoke streamed out of the toaster oven. He grumbled a curse word under his breath as he snatched the tray of biscuits out of the oven and turned on the stove top exhaust fan to suck the foul air from the house. He glared at the blackened bread and mentally kicked himself for getting so distracted by his prurient interest in Violet's love scene that he ruined their dinner.

"Gunnar?" Violet called quietly from the guest room. "Is everything okay out there? It smells like something's burning."

Yeah, me *after watching you get it on with*

the pretty boy. And yet he was oddly disturbed, too…unsettled.

"Everything's fine." He stared at the biscuits and decided he could salvage most of them by trimming the burned edges off and removing the top crust. He gave the soup a brisk stir, then ladled a bowl each for Violet and himself. After putting two of the lesser-burned biscuits on a plate, he carried her supper into the guest room on a bed tray. "Soup's on."

Violet tried to sit up, but when she moved her injured leg, she hissed in pain and collapsed weakly to the bed. "Guess I need you to help prop me up."

"Sure." Gunnar set the tray aside. When he gathered pillows from the other side of the bed to put behind Violet's back, her black cat, who'd been sleeping beside Violet, glared reprovingly at him, as if the cat knew what Gunnar had been doing ten minutes earlier. With a disgruntled feline sniff, the cat hopped down from the bed and pranced out of the room.

When Gunnar slid an arm behind Violet's

back, his skin tingled, and the image of her bare body teased his brain. Keeping his gaze averted from hers, he helped her lean forward, then stuffed two more pillows behind her so that she could sit up to eat.

Geez, he hoped his expression didn't give him away. He just needed a few minutes alone to gather his composure.

"The soup smells good. Maybe I'm hungrier than I thought," she said as he moved the legged tray to straddle her lap.

"Sorry about the bread." He waved a finger toward the biscuits and backed toward the door, eager to make his escape. "I, uh…got busy and, um, forgot to check them."

Hell. He was stammering like an idiot. *Way to keep your cool, dude.*

"They're all right. I'm not much of a cook, either."

He gritted his teeth. Somehow her being so nice about the biscuits made him feel all the guiltier about his internet fishing expedition.

"Right, so—" he wiped his hands on the seat

of his jeans as he edged toward the door "—if you need anything else…"

"Wait, you're leaving? You're not going to eat with me?"

"You…want me to eat in here?" *Brilliant, soldier. Way to state the obvious.*

"Why wouldn't you?" she asked.

A legion of moths batted their wings in his gut. "Um, no reason. I'll…be right back with my food."

He marched into the kitchen, dragging in a deep breath and trying to shake the image of Violet writhing under the boy toy out of his head. *Come on, Gunnar. Pull it together.*

He got his soup from the counter, steeled himself and headed back into the guest room, dragging a kitchen chair with him. He planted himself next to her and concentrated his attention on his soup, as if he needed all his focus on the task so he wouldn't spill it.

Violet sipped a spoonful of soup and licked the drips from her lips. "It's delicious. You said your housekeeper made this?"

"Not mine. Derek's. She cooks for Piper and Sawyer, too."

"Oh." She sipped another spoonful, then leaned her head back as if the two bites had worn her out. "Well, it's good, whoever made it."

For the next several minutes, she continued to make awkward small talk—awkward because Gunnar was terrible at idle chitchat and was gulping down his soup as fast as he could. He'd nearly reached the bottom of his bowl when she set her spoon down and sighed.

"Gunnar, is something wrong?"

He flicked a brief glance at her. "No. Why?"

"You've hardly looked at me throughout dinner. And you're awfully quiet."

He shrugged and scraped the bottom of his bowl. "Maybe I'm just the strong, silent type."

He sensed her stare, and his skin felt too tight.

"You're sure nothing's wrong? You didn't hear bad news about Mary or something?"

He darted a look at her. "No. I haven't heard anything about Mary. I swear."

She nodded, and he ducked his head, remembering the reports about Violet he'd found. "But, um…"

"But?" A note of alarm tinged her voice.

He raised a hand to calm her. "Nothing to panic over, but…rumors about you getting hurt on the set of the movie have reached the internet. Someone from the movie crew apparently reported that you went to see a doctor today and—"

She heaved a sigh. "Figures." She shook her head and fingered the edge of the sheet. "I'm so sick of being under a microscope. All my dirty laundry on display for the public."

Guilt lobbed another blow in Gunnar's gut, and his soup roiled in his stomach.

"Are you done?" He jerked his head toward her barely touched supper, and he stood with his own empty dish in hand.

"I guess. I—" She frowned. "How did you know that report had been leaked?"

His heart gave a hard thump. "Um…I saw it on—"

Violet stiffened and sat up. "Oh, my God! You checked Google!"

Gunnar froze, and a guilty flush stung his neck, his cheeks. "No!"

She narrowed a dubious glare on him. "Really?"

"I, uh—" his shoulders drooped, and he dropped back onto his chair "—yes, damn it."

She sighed. "And?"

He shot her a wary look. "And what?"

"Besides the reports of my supposed on-set injury, what did you find?" She folded her arms over her chest and settled back in the pillows.

He waved her off. "Nothing really."

"Oh? Then why won't you look at me?"

That brought his head up, his gaze darting to her. "I—"

"Something about my Oscar nomination, I hope. I'd like to think I have some good press along with the lies and rumors."

He swallowed hard and set his bowl aside. Clearly she wasn't going to let the issue drop, so he might as well man up and stop evading the truth. She deserved as much. "There was a picture of you on the red carpet. You looked beautiful. Hot, in fact."

"For a mother of twins, you mean." She plucked the sheet again and twisted her mouth skeptically.

"No, hot as in *hot*." He met her gaze squarely, drilling his message home with a hard look. "Period. You were workin' it, Tinkerbell. And the fact that you have young twins makes it all the more impressive."

"So you didn't catch the Cheerios in my hair?"

He lifted an eyebrow, intrigued. "Cheerios?"

"My publicist was good enough to point them out to me…*after* I'd walked the red carpet."

Gunnar dragged a hand over his mouth to hide a chuckle. "No. I didn't see any Cheerios, but then… I wasn't looking at your hair." He quirked an eyebrow and twitched a devilish grin.

She rolled her eyes. "What else did you find?"

He grunted and shoved to his feet. "Geez, I don't know…"

"Sit!" She aimed a finger at the chair, and her brown eyes flashed with authority.

He sent her an amused look. "Well, well...Tinkerbell the drill sergeant."

She wrinkled her nose, scowling at him. "Why do you keep calling me Tinkerbell?"

He lifted a shoulder and gratefully seized the change of topic. "Seemed to fit. When I met you, that was the impression you made."

"Because I'm short?"

"That and the pixie haircut, and the green dress and your sass...I don't know. It was the whole package. Why?"

She huffed her impatience. "It just...sounds like you're mocking me."

He feigned innocence. "Would I do that?"

She lowered her chin and glared up at him through narrowed eyes. After a few seconds, she said, "You read something about Adam's death, too, no doubt."

She'd caught him off guard, and he paused to take a breath before answering. "Yeah." He moved the bed tray out of her way, then sat back down on the edge of the chair and propped his arms on his knees. "Drug overdose?"

She shifted slightly so that she faced him. "That's what the tox screen said. I had them run it twice to be sure." Her face darkened, and she glanced down at her fidgeting fingers. "He swore to me he'd been clean since the boys were born. He'd been to rehab, straightened his life out, made his family his priority...or so he claimed."

"Wouldn't you know? Didn't you see him—?" Gunnar cut himself off abruptly, realizing how forward and painful his questions had to be. The deep V in her brow confirmed as much. "Sorry. Forget that..."

"You're right." She flipped a hand up. "I should have known. I should have. But I *wanted* to believe him. I *wanted* to trust him." Her voice cracked, and tears filled her eyes. "But he lied to me. About more than just the drugs it turns out."

Gunnar tensed, rubbed his sweaty palms on his jeans. He didn't want to go down this emotional path with her. He was hardly the warm and fuzzy confidante type, and witnessing her tears was like having a rock in his boot. "I'm sorry," he said lamely.

She dried her cheek with her finger and shook her head. "No, I'm sorry for blubbering again. I guess my defenses are low today. I'm not usually so weepy."

Gunnar wanted to get out of there, like ten minutes ago, but knew he couldn't leave now without looking like the cold bastard he probably was. It wasn't that he didn't care, didn't want to comfort her. He'd love to help her if he could. But he didn't know how.

He didn't know what to do with his own emotional baggage, so how the hell was he supposed to handle her pain?

He plucked a tissue from a box of Kleenex and held it out to her.

She took it and flashed a quick embarrassed grin. "What am I doing? You don't want to hear my sordid tale of woe."

He swallowed hard. "If you need to get it off

your chest, I'll listen. But I don't know how much help or advice I can give you."

She closed her eyes for a moment, her fingers curling into the covers at her waist. After a moment of silence, she said quietly, "Do you know how much the tabloids offered to pay me for the inside scoop concerning Adam's death, our marriage and his affair with the waitress in Denver?" She opened her eyes and sent him a sad smile. "And you think I'm going to spill it all to you for nothing?"

He raised his eyebrows, startled. "I only meant—"

Her smile brightened, though the sadness lingered in her doelike eyes. "I know. And I may take you up on your offer. Someday. But not tonight."

He tried not to let his relief show in his expression, but she was apparently too good at reading people for him to pull it off.

She hummed her amusement. "Yeah, you dodged a bullet there, didn't you, soldier?"

"And on that note…" He rose to his feet again

and moved his dirty dish onto her tray. Lifting the bed tray, he started for the door. "I think I'll take my leave. You need to sleep."

She tugged the covers higher, nestling into the sheets with a weary nod of agreement. "You'll wake me when Emma and Tate come by?"

"Of course." He caught the bottom of the door with his foot to pull it closed.

"Gunnar?"

"Yeah?"

"You do know that wasn't me, right?"

He frowned. "What?"

"The sex scene you watched before dinner."

His gut jerked tight, and adrenaline pumped through him. "Uh...what?"

"Why else would you suddenly be so nervous around me?" She sent him a smug grin. "Besides, even though you kept the volume low, I recognized the background music."

Gunnar opened his mouth but couldn't speak, didn't know what to say.

"The T and A shots? They used a body double. Had to. It's in all my contracts."

"I—" Gunnar felt an awkward heat sting his face.

"I know." She pulled a falsely crestfallen face. "Disappointing, right? But it gets worse. When we filmed that movie— and I know which scene it was, because I've only done one nude scene— I was two months' pregnant with Mason and Hudson, and I was sick as a dog. We had to stop rolling three times just during the shower scene for me to barf. Mark and I had to stay in that tight clench the whole time so my baby bump didn't show. Oh, and the guy in the scene, Mark Gilliard, had horrible halitosis, which didn't help my nausea one bit."

Gunnar realized his mouth was open, so he snapped it shut. "Um…"

What was he supposed to say to that?

She gave a short laugh. "Real sexy, huh? Sorry to disillusion you."

He blew out a deep breath and cleared his throat. "Well…wow. So there it is."

She shrugged. "Sorry. Not real."

He nodded, squared his shoulders, and met her

eyes with a hard, meaningful gaze. "Yeah, but the red carpet shot, you in the sexy blue number? *That* was real." He flashed a smoldering grin. "And you were hot."

A lopsided smile lit her face, and her cheeks flushed pink.

As he backed out the door, he gave her a wink. "Sleep well, Tinkerbell."

Chapter 6

A light knock on the bedroom door woke Violet a couple hours later. She rubbed her eyes and glanced around the unfamiliar room, trying to orient herself. The dull throb in her leg and ache in her head brought the day's events back to her in a painful rush.

The attack. Mary's cries…

The door opened, and Dr. Colton peeked in. "Violet, you awake? I'd like to check your wound and vital signs."

"Yeah, come in."

A tall, sandy-haired man and auburn-tressed woman entered behind Dr. Colton. Though she'd been traumatized, weak from blood loss and doped up on painkillers, Violet recalled meeting Dr. Colton and Gunnar's brother and sister at the medical clinic. She knew they were both in law enforcement, but still groggy from her nap, she couldn't remember their names at the moment.

"How are you feeling?" Dr. Colton asked as he set a medical bag on the end of the bed.

"Honestly? Horrible. Sore all over. Bone-tired. But glad to be alive." She gave him the best smile she could. "How are my boys?" She canted forward, eager for news about Hudson and Mason. "Did you bring them with you?"

Derek smiled warmly and shook his head. "No, we didn't bring them tonight. Last time I checked, they'd both had their baths, were in their pajamas and were playing peekaboo with Piper and a purple elephant."

Violet smiled, and a stab of longing squeezed her chest. Even after a couple of hours away from her twins, she missed their chubby faces and sweet hugs. "Did they eat well at dinner?"

Dr. Colton nodded. "Did they ever. They had mac and cheese and fruit salad. Your boys are in good hands, mama."

She sank back in the pillows, satisfied her babies were safe, even if she ached to have them with her. "Thank you for taking care of them. And thank you again for all you did today to save my life." She paused and bit her lip. "Do you think you could get word to the Amish gentlemen who helped me? I want them to know how much I appreciate what they did for me as well."

"Emma can deliver your message to Caleb Troyer," Dr. Colton said and nodded toward his sister. "He's her new boyfriend."

Emma scoffed. "Geez, Derek. You make it sound so…high school." Then looking to Violet she added, "But I will let Caleb know you send your thanks. And I'll deliver the message to Isaac Lapp, as well." She tilted her head in query. "You feel up to answering some questions when Derek is through?"

Violet nodded. "I'll do my best."

"Well, the good news is your stitches look fine. No signs of infection. And I can give you something to make you more comfortable."

Violet drew her eyebrows together and gave Derek a skeptical look. "You mean a narcotic."

"The best painkillers are narcotics. Is that a problem?" Derek turned up a palm. "That's what I gave you at the office."

Violet sighed. "Four years ago, when my career really began to take off, my husband got caught up in the party scene in Hollywood. He was already a heavy drinker, and when alcohol no longer gave him the buzz he wanted, he experimented with both prescription and illegal drugs. They were everywhere around him, and he saw no reason not to partake with his new buddies. Apparently he missed the day in school when they talked about defying peer pressure and the dangers of drugs and alcohol. His alcohol addiction became a drug addiction. He lost interest in his family, in our marriage and ten months ago, an overdose killed him." A movement at the door drew her attention. Gunnar propped a shoulder in the doorway and watched her with soulful hazel eyes. The intensity of his gaze had a more powerful effect on her than any drug she knew, burrowing deep to her marrow and warming her from her core.

"I heard about your husband's death, Violet, and I'm sorry for your loss." Dr. Colton's voice redirected her attention.

She nodded her acknowledgment of his condolences. "I don't want narcotics or anything addictive, even if it means I'm going to hurt."

Dr. Colton raised his eyebrows. "If you're sure…" He glanced to Gunnar. "You have any ibuprofen in the cabin?"

Gunnar pushed away from the door frame. "I'll check. If I don't, the pharmacy on Main Street is open twenty-four hours."

When Gunnar disappeared from view, Violet experienced an odd sense of loss, a hollow pang a lot like loneliness, which was silly since she had three other Coltons crowded in the small bedroom with her. And since she'd only known Gunnar one day. And since most of that time they'd been happily exchanging barbed gibes and pushing each other's buttons.

That was real. And you were hot. The echo of Gunnar's compliment sent a sweet shiver through her.

"You cold?" Dr. Colton asked as he palpated her wrist for her pulse.

Not according to your brother, she thought but said, "Maybe a little."

"Hey, mind if we get started? I'm supposed to meet with Caleb and the church elders in an hour," Emma said.

"You're seriously going to convert and follow Amish law?" the sandy-haired Colton brother asked. "You do realize no electricity means more than just no lightbulbs. It means no hair dryer, no dishwasher, no air conditioning…"

Emma gave her brother a classic sisterly sneer. "Yes, I know that, Tate." A confident smile tugged her mouth. "But Caleb is worth it." When she turned back to Violet, Emma tipped her head again in query. "So shall we start?"

Dr. Colton finished listening to Violet's heartbeat and stepped back, removing his stethoscope from his ears. "I'm done. You're doing great. Keep taking your antibiotic and getting as much rest as you can. I'll check in with you again tomorrow. Okay?"

Emma took a seat in the kitchen chair that Gunnar had left in the room earlier. "Let's go over your statement again from the beginning, okay? Have you remembered anything else about the attack…the vehicle the men were in, something they said?"

"Tell us everything you remember, even if it seems trivial." Tate took Dr. Colton's place at the side of the bed. "Sometimes cases are solved based on the tiniest detail."

"Well…let me think." Violet closed her eyes, dredged up the sights and sounds from earlier that morning. A dark, ominous sense of doom crawled through her, as it had when she'd realized what the men wanted and why she and Mary had been singled out. Hugging the bed covers more tightly around her shoulders to ward off the chill the memories brought, she tried to remember what she'd told Emma and Tate already. Even that was foggy, thanks to the addled state she'd been in, both physically and mentally, right after the attack.

She heard male voices—Gunnar's and Dr. Colton's—drift in from the hall, followed by the front door opening and closing and the scuff of boots returning to the guest room door. Even if she hadn't heard Gunnar's return, she'd have sensed it. She knew well the feeling of being watched, yet in Gunnar's case, having his gaze on her made her feel feminine, safe...alive.

"They parked the car at an angle in front of us, blocking our path. Even before I saw their ski masks, I knew something was wrong. I sensed their evil intent." She opened her eyes and glanced from Emma to Tate. "I know that sounds crazy—"

"Not at all," Tate assured her. "You'd be surprised how often we hear that. And how often people dismiss that sixth sense."

"I, for one, believe it is a natural born instinct,

as real as fight or flight or a mother's instinct to protect her young," Emma added.

"I relied on it many times in Afghanistan," Gunnar said, folding his arms over his chest. "Entering a new village. Meeting an unescorted car on the road. Saved my life more than once." He held her gaze for long second, until Emma cleared her throat.

"You were saying they wore ski masks. What color ski masks?"

"Black. They were some polyester knit. And they had dark coats, gloves and boots. One guy's coat was black and a little puffy, like an insulated jacket. I couldn't see his shirt. His jacket was zipped to the neck."

"You're sure it was an insulated coat? Zipped, not buttoned?" Emma asked.

Violet blinked. Thought about what she'd seen. "Yeah. Why?"

"The Amish don't use zippers or man-made fabrics."

Violet thought about that and shook her head. "No, they weren't Amish, but I think they were familiar with Amish people and traditions. The guy who grabbed me mocked my use of a curse word, saying my *Mamm* and *Datt* wouldn't like it."

Tate scribbled a note and nodded to her. "Go on."

"Well, the other guy's coat was a scratchy fabric like wool and hung longer. Past his hips. And more blue than black."

She continued describing the silver car, the men's voices, what they said, the weapons they had. She trembled remembering the shock of having her attacker's blade sink into her thigh. She told them everything she could remember doing to defend herself, blow by blow. Recounted her angry words, her attacker's taunts, her admission that she wasn't Amish.

Guilt plucked at her. If she hadn't denied the identity they'd assumed from her dress, would she be with Mary now, able to protect and defend the young woman? Would they have taken her instead and let Mary go free?

"I shouldn't have said what I did. I should have

let them believe I was Amish. Maybe if I had, Mary would—"

"No," Tate said firmly. "Don't play that game with yourself. You did what you had to. You did the right thing. How long do you think it would have been before they recognized you from the movies? Or your short hair and mannerisms gave you away? Who knows what they'd have done then."

Trembling and nauseated, Violet sucked in a deep breath, considering the truths Tate presented. If they'd killed her, Hudson and Mason would have been orphans. And Mary would still have been alone with her kidnappers.

"Tell me again what the man whose ski mask you pulled off looked like," Emma said.

"I only got a glimpse, but he had average features, brown hair, no facial hair."

Violet did her best to describe what she remembered, racking her brain for any detail that would help the FBI and police find Mary and bring her safely home. No, she didn't get any license plate numbers. No, she didn't think she'd managed to scratch her attacker or get his DNA on her. No, she didn't still have her clothes from the attack. She'd left them at Dr. Colton's office. After forty more minutes of exhausting questions, she sighed and turned up her hands. "That's all I can think of."

"I'll come by again tomorrow and let you work with the local police sketch artist. She'd have come with us today, but she was tied up with some other official business." Emma glanced to Tate. "Shall we go? Caleb's waiting for me."

Violet bid Gunnar's brother and sister goodbye and listened to the fading murmur of voices as he walked them out. When the cabin fell quiet again, she heard his footsteps approach her door. She watched the opening, waiting for him to return, and when he appeared at the threshold, her breath hitched a little. Even as physically weak and emotionally wrung out as she was, the sight of his broad shoulders and rough-hewn face stirred something elementally female inside her.

"I have that ibuprofen you wanted," he said and rattled the bottle.

"Please."

He brought the bottle of ibuprofen to her bedside, along with a glass of water, and shook two tablets into his palm. After she plucked the pills from his hand, he helped her lean up enough to sip the water and wash down the tablets.

"Gunnar?" she said, wiping a dribble from her lips with the back of her hand. "You saw some pretty horrible stuff in Afghanistan, didn't you?"

His gaze darted to hers, and his body tensed. "Why do you ask?"

"I guess I'm just wondering how you handled it. I'd imagine you saw people die, maybe even your fellow soldiers. Your friends."

His jaw tightened, and he jerked a quick nod.

Flash images of Mary, their attackers and her own blood taunted Violet. She saw the graphic pictures every time she closed her eyes and heard Mary's cries in her memory even when she was awake. "So how…how have you dealt with it?"

Gunnar pinned a grave look on her that made her shiver. "Who said I have?"

His answer startled her. "Do you still have nightmares about your tour of duty?"

His brow furrowed, and he hesitated, studied her, as if deciding whether to trust her, whether he should open that can of worms. "Let's just say," he began, his tone pitched low, "I have a few things I'm still working through."

Without thinking about why or if she should, Violet reached for his hand and curled her fingers around his. The expression that passed over his face told her she'd startled him with the gesture, but she held tight to his hand, needing the connection, wanting the comfort she derived merely from his presence.

"So…no tips on how to make the sights and sounds go away?"

He sat down on the edge of the guest bed, and his hip nudged hers. "Wish I did. People keep telling me it takes time. Time to put some distance from what happened and put it behind me." He shrugged. "I've been home for six months."

Her mouth felt dry, despite the water she'd just sipped. "And?"

He twisted his mouth in thought. "Apparently six months isn't long enough." He met her gaze, and his expression softened. "Would you like me to stay until you fall asleep?"

His kind offer burrowed deep inside her and tangled with all the dark, troubled feelings the day had brought. "Would you? I mean…I feel a little silly asking. I know I'm safe here, but…"

"Don't give it another thought." He sent her a small lopsided grin, and her heart staggered.

When he smiled, Gunnar Colton's rugged features were transformed into a breath-stealing vision of raw male sensuality.

Oh, no, no, no, Violet chided herself. *Do* not *go there.* Her life was in enough chaos with this morning's attack, Mary's kidnapping, the stalled movie production, clamoring paparazzi at every turn and—oh, yeah—twin boys to raise alone after her husband's drug overdose. The last thing she needed in her life now was a mercurial ex-elite forces soldier with his own baggage to sort out.

Even as the warnings tripped through her brain, Gunnar shifted his grip, lacing their fingers and giving her hand a squeeze. "Close your eyes, and think about those boys of yours. Think about the sound of their laughter."

She did as he suggested, and a smile found her lips.

"Now try to sleep. I'll be right here."

His deep voice rolled through her like a warm wave at the seashore. But his promise not to leave brought her the most comfort and peace of all.

Chapter 7

On Tuesday morning, Gunnar was still drinking his morning coffee, clad only in his sleep pants, when a knock on his front door heralded Derek's arrival with Violet's twins. Gunnar groaned under his breath, took one more fortifying gulp of caffeine and shuffled to the door to let Derek in.

"Morning," Derek said, sweeping into the living room and depositing a large blue bag with a smiling giraffe on his sofa and an apple-cheeked baby with curls the color of honey on the floor. "How'd Violet do last night?"

Gunnar shrugged. "Okay. She didn't sleep too

well, but her leg isn't showing any signs of infection."

"Good." Derek nodded to the baby. "This is Hudson. You have to keep a close eye on him. He's real active and into everything." He sounded out of breath as he hurried back to the door. "I'll be right back with Mason. He's still in my car."

With that, Derek disappeared out the front door. Gunnar eyed the toddler, and Hudson stared back up at him with wide curious brown eyes, every bit as doelike as his mother's. Dread knotted Gunnar's stomach as he and the toddler sized each other up.

"Ma?" the tyke said, lifting a hand and wiggling his fingers.

His gut twisted tighter. Did that mean the kid needed something?

Derek bustled through the door again, toting a carbon copy of the first baby, down to his identical red shirt and elastic-waisted blue jeans, and a portable crib. "And this is Mason. Everything you should need is in the diaper bag including written instructions from their nanny." He set the collapsed crib by the front door. "They'll nap together in this when the time comes. It's pretty simple to set up. You shouldn't have any problems. Try not to bother Violet with lots of questions. She needs to rest. And don't let her boys see her or they'll be clamoring to get to her. The last thing she needs, with her injuries, is boisterous toddlers climbing on her and demanding her attention." Derek backed out the door. "Piper will stop by to pick them up after school. Good luck."

As Derek stepped out on the porch, panic swamped Gunnar. "Hey, wait! That's it? That's all the directions I get?"

"Sorry, I'm already running late. You'll be fine. Tell Violet I'll check on her again tonight." Derek tried to close the door, but Gunnar caught the knob and pulled it open again.

"Derek, I have no idea what to do with them. You know I have no experience with babies." Gunnar tried to keep the apprehension out of his voice, but even he heard the tension threading his tone.

Laughing, Derek continued walking backward toward his idling car. "God, I wish I had a picture of your face right now. In fact…" Derek pulled out his cell phone and aimed it at Gunnar.

Gunnar shot him a scowl and quickly closed the door before Derek could snap a picture to tease him with later.

The babies sat side by side, grinning at each other and taking in their new environment with curious eyes. How was he supposed to tell them apart? And did it really matter? Mason—or was that Hudson?—spotted the diaper bag on the sofa and pulled himself to his feet. With a chubby grabbing hand, he yanked the strap of the bag and toppled it to its side. A small cup that had been in a side pocket rolled out, and with a squeal of delight, Mason—or maybe it was Hudson—seized the container and shook it with glee. Something inside rattled loudly.

"Whatcha got there, buddy?" Gunnar sat on the edge of the couch and took the container with the snap-on lid from the kid to look inside.

The toddler loosed a wail that would wake the

dead. Gunnar shuddered, then clapped a hand over the toddler's mouth. "Geez, kid. Pipe down. You want to wake your mother?"

The kid wiggled free with a strength that surprised Gunnar, and chubby hands grabbed for the container. "Chee-oos!"

Not wanting to get into a tug-of-war with a baby, he let the boy have the plastic bowl. "Fine. Have it. Whatever."

Plopping down on his diaper-padded butt, the blond cherub pried the lid off and, in the process, flung dry cereal across the floor.

Gunnar groaned. "Great. A mess already."

The second boy cooed with obvious delight and crawled over to start munching the cereal straight from the floor.

"Hey, no!" Gunnar tried to grab the cereal from the kid's slobbery fingers, then hesitated. Sighed. "Oh, well. A little dirt is good for you. Right?"

While the twins sat at his feet, sharing the cereal and occasionally feeding it to each other and giggling about it, Gunnar fished out the directions from the nanny and scanned the sheet.

Snack at 10:00 a.m. Lunch at 12:00 p.m. Nap at 1:00 p.m. Snack at 3:00 p.m.

Ointment for Mason's diaper rash is in side pocket.

"Diaper rash?" Gunnar sent the babies a look of horror. He had to change diapers?

Fingers gripping the instructions harder, Gunnar read on, *Hudson gets one teaspoon of his antibiotic every four hours and decongestant syrup every six hours.*

"Crap. Medicine? That means I have to figure out which of you is which." He stared at the twins and tried to find some distinguishing feature. But to his eye, the kids were exact duplicates. "Okay. Let's try this…Mason?"

Both heads came up and turned to blink at him. Strike one.

Gunnar thought about it some more. In high school, they'd played shirts and skins to distinguish teams for basketball. Picking up the closest baby, he headed back to Violet's room, then remembered Derek's warning not to let the boys see their mother. He knocked on Violet's door, and after getting permission to enter, he opened the door a crack.

Holding the baby behind the door out of view, he peered inside. Violet looked rumpled and groggy, her sheets a tangled mess and the bruises on her face a darker shade of purple this morning. "Hey, sorry to disturb you. Derek thought it would be best if your kids didn't know you were here, but I need your help. Which one is this?"

He put his hand over the boy's eyes and moved to where Violet could see the baby tucked under his arm like a football.

Violet's face lit up when she saw her son, and she pushed awkwardly to a seated position for a better view. "Hudson," she mouthed.

"Roger that. I'll be back with your breakfast in a minute. You need more ibuprofen?"

She nodded and lay back, her eyes widening as she took in his dishabille. Oops. Maybe he should put on a shirt before he came back with her breakfast.

Gunnar returned to the living room, pulling off Hudson's shirt—Hudson would be skins—and found that Mason had ransacked the diaper bag in the short time he'd been out of sight. Diapers and toys, toddler cups and baggies of snacks were scattered everywhere. Putting Hudson on the floor, he scowled at Mason, who looked pretty pleased with his handiwork, and began gathering the strewn items. He moved the diaper bag out of the toddlers' reach and dragged a hand through his hair. Now what?

Violet needed ibuprofen and breakfast. The boys needed something safe to occupy them. He opened the bag and took out two stuffed animals. After giving one to each baby, he aimed a finger at them. "Play with those toys, and don't get into anything. I'll be right back."

Gunnar hurried out of the living room and found a muffin for Violet, poured her some coffee and put two ibuprofen on the tray next to her breakfast. Happy giggles and squeals drifted in from the living room. Good. At least they weren't crying. Crying meant something bad had happened, right?

Just the same, he walked a little faster delivering the tray to Violet. "Here ya go. Breakfast, pills and coffee. Anything else?"

"Um, yeah." She gave him a tentative look, her attention to his chest reminding him he'd neglected to get a shirt. "Can you help me get to the bathroom? I need to go, and it hurts to put too much weight on my leg."

He rubbed his hands on his pajama pants and moved to the side of the bed. "Sure."

Gunnar helped her sit up, swing her feet to the floor and rise on her good leg. Stooping low to accommodate her short stature, he kept an arm under her as she hobble-hopped toward the bathroom. After several seconds of this painstaking process, Gunnar grunted, "Screw this."

He swept her into his arms and carried her the rest of the way down the hall and set her on her feet in the bathroom. "Call me when you're done."

He backed out, closing the door behind him

and trying not to think about how perfectly she'd fit in his arms, how good it felt to have her nestled against his chest and her hands on his skin as she clung to him.

Dragging in a cleansing breath, he returned to the living room to check on the twins. The stuffed animals had been abandoned, and the boys, both stripped down to their diapers, had toddled over to his fireplace and were digging through last weekend's ashes as if it were a sandbox. Soot covered his floor and Violet's imps from head to toe.

Gunnar sighed. It was going to be a long day.

"Thanks," Violet said as Gunnar carried her back to the guest bed. "I hope the boys aren't giving you too much trouble."

"Define too much," he grumbled.

She noticed that Gunnar had pulled on a T-shirt while she was in the restroom, and a pang of disappointment plucked at her. He had an impressive chest and ripped abs, and it seemed a shame to cover all that muscled male beauty.

She studied his frown as he propped pillows under her injured leg and tugged her covers over her. "Uh-oh. What did they do?" She spotted black smudges on his cheek and knitted her brow. "What's on you face?"

"Soot. They got in the fireplace."

She tensed. "What!"

Gunnar raised both hands, palms out. "It wasn't lit. But I have to give them both a bath now and vacuum my living room." He heaved a sigh and shot her an exasperated look. "They've only been here thirty minutes, and they've already worn me out. How do you do it?"

Violet chuckled. "I have help. Rani is a miracle worker." She sobered a bit and caught his hand to make sure she had his full attention. "Thank you. I know this is not what you signed on for."

"I didn't sign on for anything, Tinkerbell." He blew out a breath and rolled the kinks from his shoulders. "But you're welcome. Any hints you have for keeping the Lost Boys occupied and out of trouble would be appreciated." He held his finger and thumb so that they nearly touched. "I'm this close to hog-tying them to a chair."

She didn't miss the Peter Pan reference but let it slide. Apparently that was his theme for nicknames for her family. "Believe me, I've been tempted to do that myself more than once." She brushed her hair off her forehead, then tipped her head. "Get on the floor with them and play. They love blocks and wrestling and trains. When you've had all that you can stand, they should have a DVD in their bag. They love *Baby Einstein*."

"Blocks and *Baby Einstein*. Check." He gave her an appraising glance. "How about you? You good for a while? I'm about to be up to my armpits bathing sooty babies."

"Yeah, I'm good." He headed for the door, and she added, "Oh, and Gunnar, don't leave them alone in the bathtub—even for a second. Okay?"

He gave her a thumbs-up. "Roger that."

He left the door partially open, and Violet sank into the pillow and stared up at the ceiling, listening to Gunnar's voice and her children's bab-bling and squawks filter down the hall.

"Okay, dudes. Bath time."

"Baff?"

"Hey, don't put that in your mouth. That's dis-gusting."

Put what in his mouth? She bit her lip and tried not to worry. Her boys were fine. Gunnar could handle things.

And yet…Hudson and Mason were a handful at the best of times, and Gunnar had no experi-ence with babies. It only took a second for a di-saster to happen.

The thud of footsteps drew her attention to the sliver of hall she could see through the open door. As Gunnar passed the guest room, she glimpsed her boys, one in each of his arms.

"No baff!" Mason whined.

She wanted more than anything to call Gun-nar back and ask him to bring her babies to her. But Derek's suggestion was spot on. It was best the boys didn't know she was there, or they'd give Gunnar fits crying to be with her and trying to climb on the bed to cuddle. She was still bone tired and hurt all over, and her leg throbbed mercilessly whenever she moved too much. Letting her rambunctious toddlers climb on her and tug at her for attention was not conducive to her healing.

But she missed her sweet boys so much...

The whoosh of water filling a bathtub rumbled down the hall, and she heard Hudson, her adventurer, squeal with delight.

"Here you go, sport. It's okay. Look, your brother likes it."

Violet closed her eyes and could picture more cautious Mason clinging to Gunnar's arm and eyeing the unfamiliar bathtub with suspicion. But as soon as Mason realized Hudson was loving the bath, he followed his brother's lead.

She wasn't sure why she felt so at ease allowing a man who'd seemed so hostile and intimidating the first time she'd met him take charge of her children's care. Maybe because he'd shown her such gentle attentiveness through a rough night. She'd awakened often, hurting and unable to shake the haunting images of her attackers, and Gunnar had been right beside her, just as he'd promised, to calm her, to fetch her more medicine, to reassure her she was safe. He'd slept in the hard wooden chair from the kitchen, and when she urged him to sleep somewhere more comfortable, he'd insisted he was fine.

"I learned to sleep under the worst conditions in Afghanistan. If I get too comfy in my bed, I might not hear you when you need me."

The translation was he was sacrificing his comfort to take care of her. Violet recognized that truth with humbling gratitude. But then, wasn't that what all soldiers did? Sacrifice their comfort, their safety, their lives so that the people they loved back home would be safe, so that even strangers in a foreign land could be protected?

And Gunnar had served for eleven years....

Her respect for him, despite his occasional grumpiness, grew every time she saw a new side of him.

Let's just say I have a few things I'm still working through.

Violet's heart clenched with concern for Gunnar. What kind of horrors had he witnessed in the war? On the heels of her sympathy for the issues he was still wrestling with, a voice in her head warned her not to get tangled up with another man battling personal demons. When they'd married, she'd been sure she could help Adam work through his problems, that her love would be the magic key to fixing his addictive behavior and the issues behind his alcohol abuse. Violet sighed heavily, acknowledging how naive and foolishly optimistic she'd been.

Lesson learned. No more men with complex emotional baggage for her.

That decision should have made her feel stronger and more confident about her future. So why did she feel a pang of disappointment, as if this safeguard meant she'd be losing something wonderful?

"Hey, take it easy, guys. I'll get my bath later. Stop—" Gunnar sputtered as, clearly, he got a face full of bathwater. "Oh, nice shot. But let's keep some of the water in the tub, okay? I don't have flood insurance."

Violet smiled, picturing the scene she knew well. Gunnar was being a good sport considering she and her boys had invaded his private sanctuary, imposed on his hospitality and burdened him with nurse and nanny duty.

And then the earlier pang made sense. If she kept Gunnar and his problems at arm's length, she'd miss out on knowing the incredible man beneath the gruff yet oh-so-sexy exterior. And that would be a loss, indeed.

Tate Colton stacked lunch meat, pickles and cheese on a roll in the kitchen of the ranch house and was just about to bite into his Dagwood sandwich when his cell phone buzzed. Giving his lunch a wistful look, he set the massive sandwich back on his plate and answered the call.

"Colton here."

"Tate, Solomon Miller is finally cooperating." Recognizing his boss's voice, Tate shoved the plate aside and focused on what Hugo Villanueva was saying. "He's giving us names associated with the online sex ring and locations where the girls are being held. I need you to be ready to move on this soon."

"Of course. What's the plan?"

"I want you undercover, posing as a buyer. Since the sex ring seems to be targeting wealthy men with the funds to pay top dollar for these girls, you'll tell people you're a rich businessman from New York City. I'll be in touch with law enforcement in New York and New Jersey to let them know what we're doing and get the proper approvals."

"Rich businessman, huh? The department gonna bankroll this?" Tate rubbed his chin and frowned. Budget cuts already had the police department handcuffed, and undercover operations could get pricy, especially if he wanted to appear as wealthy as he would pretend to be.

"I'll talk to the mayor about underwriting the expenses. I'd hate to let these bastards get away simply cause we couldn't fund the op."

Tate plucked at the sesame seeds on his sandwich roll and twisted his mouth in a thoughtful moue. "Let me talk to my brother. He's come into a small fortune recently and is looking for ways to pay it forward. Maybe we won't have to bug the mayor."

"Works for me. Let me know what he says."

"Sure. So when do I start?" Tate asked.

"Maybe next week or soon after. Once the details are ironed out. Be on standby."

"Got it." Energy pumped through Tate as he disconnected—the thrill of the chase, a readiness to get to work. He couldn't wait to nail the bastards involved in this online sex ring to the wall.

Chapter 8

By the time Piper showed up after school to relieve him of nanny duty, Gunnar was exhausted. He'd never seen two more active, mischievous, time-consuming babies in his life. Though to be fair, he'd never spent more than a few minutes around any baby since Piper joined the family as a toddler. He'd missed most of Sawyer's childhood while in the army.

"How'd it go?" his youngest sister asked as she hoisted one of the twins—Mason, Gunnar thought—onto her hip and nuzzled his nose.

Gunnar arched an eyebrow and draped the diaper bag strap over Piper's shoulder. "Look at my living room and you tell me."

She leaned through the front door, and her eyes widened. "Geez, Gunnar. What happened?"

"Hurricane Hudson happened, followed by a swift strike from the pillaging army of Mason the destroyer."

Piper had the audacity to laugh. Gunnar growled at her.

"Before tomorrow, you should baby-proof the cabin. It will make things easier on you."

"Tomorrow," he groaned. "I have to do this again tomorrow?"

"Cheer up. Only a few days until the weekend, and then it'll be Thanksgiving break, and I can watch them full-time." She smoothed the toddler's riotous curls back from his face.

"Definitely something to give thanks for." He felt a tug on the leg of his jeans and looked down to find the other imp peering at him with his mother's brown eyes. Sticky hands reached for him.

"Up."

Gunnar returned his attention to Piper. "What do you mean by baby-proof?"

"You know, move breakable things out of reach, put those plastic plugs in electric outlets, locks on cabinets where you store poisonous stuff."

Poisons? A shiver ran down his back. Hell, he hadn't thought about all the potentially deadly stuff under his kitchen sink and in his storage closet. Bug sprays, cleaning products, lighter fluid…

"Rearranging furniture to create a more contained and safe play area…things like that."

Gunnar rubbed his jaw and studied his living room layout. "Yeah, I can do that."

Tug, tug. "Up!"

"Hudson wants you to pick him up," Piper said with a meaningful nod to the gremlin pulling on his jeans.

"Uh…yeah, I knew that," he lied and lifted the boy to his hip. "How'd you get so smart about babies?"

"Home ec class, babysitting Sawyer, paying attention around parents of little kids." She pulled a face. "It's not rocket science, Gunnar."

"Could have fooled me," he mumbled under his breath.

He tailed Piper out to the Suburban and followed her lead as she buckled Mason into one of the car seats. Hudson had other ideas and wiggled to get free. "So where do I get these plugs for the outlets and cabinet locks you mentioned?"

Piper chuckled. "It's really sad how out of touch you are, big brother."

He cocked one eyebrow and sent Piper a disgruntled look. "Baby-proofing gear was hardly relevant in my squad's bunker. Now if you want to quiz me on disassembling an M-16 to clean sand from it or the geopolitical differences between the nomadic tribes in Afghanistan and which ones are NATO allies, then we'll talk."

Piper reached over and helped contain Hudson long enough to snap his car seat strap in place. "But you're home now. M-16s are not relevant in Eden Falls. Making sure Violet Chastain's babies don't die is."

The woman and her son lay dead in the street, covered with debris and blood...

Gunnar's breath caught, and he blinked hard to clear the image from his head. When he glanced back up at Piper, she was watching him with the same wary concern she'd had when he'd freaked out on her in town on Sunday.

"You okay?" she asked. "You've got that funny look in your eyes again."

He cleared his throat. "I'm fine. Just tell me where to buy the stuff I need to baby-proof the cabin."

"You know, Derek thinks you should talk to a counselor. He thinks you've got PTSD."

Clenching his teeth, Gunnar backed out of the SUV and closed the door. "I'm familiar with Derek's theories. But I'm okay. I just need time to make the transition to being home. I need quiet and privacy to decompress."

He started back to the porch to retrieve the portable crib, and Piper dogged his steps.

"It's been six months, Gunnar."

He shoved the collapsed and compacted crib at her. "Don't nag."

"I'm just worried about you. We all are."

Gunnar sucked in a breath and blew it out slowly. "I know, and I appreciate your concern. But I'm okay. Really I am."

Rather than voice the disagreement obvious in her expression, Piper set the crib on the ground and threw herself against him in an unexpected hug. "Love you."

He kissed the top of her head and gave her a squeeze. "Back attcha, smarty-pants."

She pulled away and sauntered back to the Suburban without the crib. "Rani thinks it will be easier to just leave the portable crib at your place. They have regular cribs at the main house."

He nodded. "Whatever."

She climbed in the driver's side of the SUV and sent him a crooked grin. "Any department store that carries baby stuff will have all the baby-proofing things you'll need."

He gave her a thumbs-up as she backed down his driveway.

An hour later, Tate arrived with the local police sketch artist in tow to work with Violet on a composite of her attacker. While Violet was occupied and Tate could keep tabs on her, Gunnar took the opportunity to drive into town to shop for baby-proofing equipment. The sheer volume of safety equipment and gadgets was mind-boggling, and rather than miss something essential, Gunnar bought several of every item.

Back at the cabin, he unloaded the bags of safety booty from his car and called down the short hall toward Violet's room. "I'm back."

Ready to be fed, Violet's black cat, Sophie, wound around his legs, making him stumble as he brought in the last load. "Yeah, yeah, in a minute. Cool it."

"Who are you talking to?"

Gunnar jerked his gaze toward the door where Tate stood, his hands in his pockets.

"Oh, uh…the cat," Gunnar admitted with a grimace.

"Hmm. I'd comment on what your hermit lifestyle is doing to your social skills if you're talking to cats, but...I have a favor to ask." Tate stepped over to the table where Gunnar had deposited the many bags from the store and peeked in one. "What's all this?"

"Piper told me I needed to baby-proof the cabin. Apparently there are endless ways a kid can get maimed or killed in the average household. Who knew?"

Tate pulled a package out of a bag. "What's this for?"

Gunnar studied the device in his brother's hand. "I have no idea."

Tate smirked, and Gunnar returned a scowl. "Watch it, or I'll have you up here tonight helping me install all this crap." He paused and glanced toward Violet's room. "Is she done with the artist?"

Tate pulled another box from the shopping bags and turned the lock kit over in his hands. "Yeah. He left a few minutes ago."

"So you have a composite for the guy who stabbed her?"

"A rough one. She only got a quick look at the side of his face, but it's a start. More than we had before." Tate glanced toward Violet's door. "She was pretty worn out when we finished. Said to tell you she was going to nap."

Gunnar nodded. "You mentioned a favor?"

Tate's expression sobered. "Yeah, it's related to the investigation into the kidnappings and on-line sex ring."

Gunnar's hand stilled on the bag he was unpacking. Mention of the crimes Tate was working sent a ripple of disgust through his gut. "Name it. If I can help bring that scum to justice, I'm in."

"You haven't heard what I want yet."

"Doesn't matter. If it's in my power to help, you've got it."

Tate cocked his head and eyed his brother skeptically. "Even giving me a few million dollars to fund an undercover operation?"

Gunnar's eyes widened. "A few million? What kind of op are you doing?"

"Villanueva is sending me undercover as a wealthy New York bigwig. It's the rich guys who can afford the fees the sex ring is charging. I'll need to dress the part, have cash available, plus enough to pay rent on a posh apartment in uptown—"

Gunnar waved a hand to stop Tate. "Done. No justification needed. I trust you. Just tell me where to transfer the money."

Tate blinked twice, then grinned. "I think I like having a billionaire for a brother."

Grunting, Gunnar continued unpacking. "I'm still getting used to the idea. It's kinda surreal." He tossed Tate a safety latch for a cabinet door. "Now about installing these gizmos…"

Tate stayed for another ninety minutes, helping Gunnar sort the baby-proofing items and installing those devices they deemed most important. After Tate left, Gunnar checked on Violet, who was still sleeping, then heated a microwaveable dinner he found in his freezer. He carried the tray of fried chicken and mashed potatoes to his recliner and turned the television on with the volume low. Setting his meal on a lamp stand by his chair, he headed back into the kitchen for a beer. When he returned to the den, he settled in his chair and retrieved his dinner…and blinked. The fried chicken breast was gone.

"What the…?" He glanced around his chair, puzzled, and spotted Romeo on the floor, chowing down on the chicken. "Hey, you little thief!" Gunnar pushed out of his chair to capture the cat, but Romeo grabbed the chicken in his mouth and ran. Gritting his teeth, he chased after the cat. "Give me my chicken, furball!"

Was it not enough that he'd spent the day running after Violet's children? Now even her cats were stirring up trouble for him.

When he finally caught Romeo and pried the chicken from the cat's mouth, he stood in the center of his den and snorted a laugh thinking about dinner-stealing cats, toddler mayhem and an injured movie star in his guest room. So much for the peace and quiet he'd thought he'd have in his cabin this winter.

He returned to his recliner, switched the television from the news channel to ESPN and tucked into his dinner. Despite the cat slobber on his meat, he devoured his food. Who knew babysitting toddlers could be so exhausting and create such an appetite?

Gunnar finished his meal while watching a college basketball match-up, but the game didn't hold his attention. His thoughts drifted frequently to the sex ring case Tate and Emma were working. Knowing the critical part Violet played in the investigation raised Gunnar's blood pressure. When the sketch of the kidnapper was released to the public, the men who'd attacked her would know who'd provided the information. As the cops' key witness, she had a huge target on her back, and he'd inherited the job of keeping her safe.

But during the bombing in the Afghan market, he hadn't protected his buddies, the Afghan woman and her child. What if he failed Violet or her children, as well? And what had happened to the quiet, safe Eden Falls he'd known growing up?

With a restless sigh, he used the remote to flip through the channels. When he came across a sexy commercial, Gunnar was reminded of the movie clip of Violet he'd seen during his internet search. His fingers tightened around the remote, and he gritted his teeth. Even if the butt and breast shots were of a body double as she claimed, the heat level of the scene and the fuel to his imagination were real enough. Gunnar rubbed his eyes with his thumbs and tried to squelch the thrum of his libido. Violet was in no position physically or emotionally to have a fling with him, and since he was in no condition to start a relationship, anything more than a fling was out of the question. Violet would be out of his cabin and moving on with her life and her acting career in a few more days, so harboring any ideas about getting close to her were pointless.

But try as he might, thoughts of Violet taunted

him. When his channel surfing brought him to a rerun of a movie in which Violet had had a small walk-on part, he watched the lame chick flick for thirty minutes, waiting for the quick glimpse of Violet as a waitress in a diner.

Finally she sauntered on screen in the short waitress uniform, and Gunnar paused the image with his DVR and stared for a moment, wondering what it was about the short, sassy actress that got under his skin. From the time he'd met her, the day her bus had been blocking his driveway, something about Violet Chastain had burrowed past his defenses and poked his peace of mind.

In the stillness of his cabin, Gunnar sighed and sank back in his recliner. He glanced around him at the sparsely decorated room and bare walls, and for the first time since his return from Afghanistan, he saw the minimalist decor as something other than efficient and clean. Despite the billions of dollars in his bank account, he had very little stuff—which was fine. He was far from materialistic. He'd gotten used to living lean and traveling light while in the military.

But had he taken his spartan decorating too far? Was his empty cabin a metaphor for his life? He lived within half a mile of his family now, yet most days, he chose to stay secluded in his little cabin, by himself. For the past couple days, though, having Violet under his roof, he'd felt… more alive and content than he had in years.

He was mulling over that realization when he heard the guest bed creak and what sounded like a gasp of pain. Hastily setting the remote aside, Gunnar shot out of his chair and hurried to check on Violet. Though the room was dark, light from the hall spilled onto the bed when he opened the door. Violet was on her side with her back to him, but she rolled toward him enough that she could meet his gaze with a slight turn of her head.

"Did I wake you?" he asked.

"No. A bad dream did that a few minutes ago. I can't stop thinking about the face the sketch artist drew this afternoon."

"I thought I heard you gasp, like you'd hurt yourself."

She gave a short, mirthless laugh and rubbed a hand on her injured leg. "There's that, too. When I turned over, trying to get comfortable, I think I pulled a stitch in my leg."

"Rethinking that painkiller yet, Tinkerbell?" he asked leaning against the door frame.

She sighed heavily. "No. My reasons for not wanting anything narcotic stand."

"How about dinner?"

"Not hungry."

He hummed his acknowledgment, though her lack of appetite bothered him. "I'll be right back."

"Would you—"

He disappeared from her door before she could finish, and a hollow feeling plucked her chest—disappointment, loneliness, maybe even a tiny bit of fear. She knew she was safe in Gunnar's cabin, but the recounting of her ordeal for the police sketch artist left her off balance.

And she missed her boys. Lying alone in the dark room made it easy to feel sorry for herself, and she hated that she seemed to be slipping into that sort of funk.

"Here you go." Gunnar swept into the room, set a glass down on the bedside stand and turned on a small lamp. "Ibuprofen and a glass of warm milk."

"Does that really work? Warm milk to help you sleep?"

"Depends what you chase it with, I suppose." He flashed her a lopsided grin that warmed her core more than any hot drink could. She was ridiculously glad that he'd returned so quickly, and she refused to examine her reasons why.

Using her arms to push, she tried to wiggle into a sitting position, only to have Gunnar put his hands under her armpits and lift her into place. He handed her the milk and dropped two pills in her palm. After swallowing the ibuprofen and washing them down with a few sips of milk, she handed him the glass. "So Tate stayed for a while to visit? I heard voices earlier along with a lot of banging and clatter."

"Oh, yeah. He helped me install some of the baby-proofing gadgets I bought tonight."

Violet cocked her head, stunned. "You baby-proofed the place? For my boys?"

He shrugged. "Seemed the prudent thing to do."

"But…they're only going to be here a few more days. Rani should be over the worst of her flu by next week and can take over watching them again."

Another lift of his shoulder. "So they'll be safer for those few days."

"It just seems like a lot of trouble and expense for a few days."

He flipped a hand casually. "Can you really put a price on safety and peace of mind?"

Her chest filled with a warmth that had nothing to do with the milk she'd sipped. Gunnar's thoughtfulness amazed her, touched her. "Thank you."

Gunnar shifted awkwardly. "Well…the way I see it, they have me outnumbered and, at times, until I get a hang of this babysitting gig, outfoxed. Baby-proofing was a tactical move. Makes it a fairer fight."

She chuckled, then sent him a dubious grin. "Was today that bad?"

"Let's just say I can't remember being this tired after a full day of special ops training."

"Mmm-hmm. And you questioned my hiring a nanny to help me with my twins…"

He opened his mouth as if to protest, but his expression said he knew he'd been bested. He shuffled back to the door. "Call me if you need anything."

She nodded, trying to ignore the flutter of uneasiness that stirred at her core as he disappeared into the hall. The day had been long and tedious, confined to bed and coping with her aching leg while Gunnar handled her rowdy children. The night ahead promised to be no less lonely, but she hated to impose on Gunnar for his company. After a crazy day with her twins, Gunnar deserved the night off to relax.

But all the rationalizations in the world didn't calm the restlessness and haunting images that threatened. The only thing that helped still the wings of panic beating inside her was knowing Gunnar was nearby.

Chapter 9

The second and third days cooped up in Gunnar's cabin went much the same as the first. Gunnar brought her breakfast, bright and early, and she passed the daylight hours shifting uncomfortably in bed and listening to her children run Gunnar ragged. Too often, her mind drifted to the police sketch of the man who'd attacked her and who still held Mary captive. Unwilling to dwell uselessly on those unsettling thoughts, she sought distraction in anything she could—crossword puzzles, studying lines she knew would likely be changed for *Wrongfully Accused,* making lists on the side margin of the newspaper of what she wanted to buy the twins for Christmas.

Every now and then, Gunnar stuck his head in her room to ask if she needed anything or to ask a babysitting question. Could the twins eat peanut butter? What did Mason want when he repeated, "na-nee, na-nee?"

"That's how he says Rani. I guess he's wondering where Rani is," she said in answer to the last question.

Gunnar jerked a nod and headed back toward the living room.

"Do they ask for me?" she asked before he could get away.

He gave her a crooked grin. "Only every ten minutes. You want me to bring them back to see you?"

Violet bit her bottom lip, tempted to say yes. But her leg gave a throb, reminding her why that was a bad idea—not to mention the fit they'd throw when Gunnar tried to take them back to the living room. Better her boys didn't see her again until she was more physically able to help

Gunnar with them. With a sinking heart, she shook her head. "Probably shouldn't."

She tried reading the magazines Piper had sent over for her in the twins' diaper bag, but the dry news journal didn't hold her interest and the gossip rag only annoyed her with its conjecture and rumor-based reports. By the third evening, she was thoroughly bored and itching to get out of bed. When she tried to use the restroom on her own, however, she discovered she was still far weaker than she'd imagined, and the wound in her thigh was still frightfully sore.

Gunnar found her leaning against the wall in the hallway, grimacing in pain. Scowling his chastisement for not calling him for help, he scooped her in his arms to carry her back to the bed.

"Thanks. I…I thought I'd regained more strength and didn't want to bother you. You've been so busy today with the boys and all…" She fumbled as he pulled the covers back over her.

"Derek called to say said he'd be by in a little

while to check on you" was Gunnar's only reply. "You need anything before then?"

Your company, she thought but shook her head.

As promised, Derek stopped by just before the dinner hour with Sawyer in tow.

"Mind if my assistant observes?" Derek asked, placing a hand on his younger brother's shoulder.

"Your assistant, huh?" Violet smiled at the boy. "You want to be a doctor when you grow up?"

Sawyer shrugged. "That or a cop like Tate."

"Both are admirable careers, and you've got great role models." She nodded her permission to Derek, and he squeezed Sawyer's shoulder before moving to the side of the bed to check Violet's leg.

She sent a quick glance to the door where Gunnar watched and waited. If Gunnar was bothered that Sawyer showed no interest in following in his footsteps, he didn't show it.

"What do you think, Squirt?" Derek asked Sawyer as he stood back to give the boy a chance to look at her stitched leg. "Will she live?"

"Cool!" Sawyer said, his eyes bright with interest and enthusiasm. "That's even more stitches than Henry Collier had when he wrecked his skateboard and busted his face up."

"Uh, yeah." Derek pulled a face, then continued patiently. "I also used a different method of closing Henry's laceration, because cosmetics were important."

"Cosmetics? You mean, like makeup?"

"Meaning his mother insisted I minimize the appearance of the scar. For Violet's wound, stopping the bleeding and closing the wound quickly to save her life were paramount."

Sawyer wrinkled his nose. "What's paramount mean?"

"One of the oldest and biggest film production companies in Hollywood," Violet quipped.

Derek grinned at her, and she heard Gunnar's humored grunt from the door.

"Huh?" Sawyer looked thoroughly confused.

"Sorry. Bad joke," she said, squeezing the boys hand. "Paramount means it is most important."

Derek pulled the covers back over her leg. "The wound is healing well. No signs of infection. Gunnar tells me you tried to put weight on it today, and it didn't go well."

"Oh, he did, did he?" She sent Gunnar an irritated look, which he met with an unrepentant quirk of his eyebrow.

"But you had the right idea," Derek said. "I want you to start using the leg again a little at a time. Just have Gunnar help steady you until you get strong again."

"Can I check her blood pressure?" Sawyer asked.

Again Derek deferred to her. "Do you mind being a guinea pig for my apprentice?"

She gave Sawyer a grave look. "No needles, right?"

Sawyer's shoulders slumped. "Naw. Derek won't let me stick people until I'm really in medical school."

Violet sent the boy a wink and a grin. "Probably a good idea." She offered her arm, pushing up her sleeve. "But you may take my take my blood pressure."

As Sawyer situated the cuff, Derek asked, "Do you remember what that device is called?"

Sawyer twisted his mouth in thought. "Sphyg—sphygameter?"

"Close. Sphygmomanometer." Derek helped him adjust the cuff, then stepped back to let Sawyer work.

"Sphygmomanometer," Sawyer repeated awkwardly.

"Now spell it," Gunnar said.

Sawyer cast his oldest brother a withering look. "You spell it!"

"I'm not the doctor-in-training."

Violet suppressed a laugh as Gunnar's little brother finished taking her blood pressure. She tried to imagine what Hudson and Mason would be like when they grew up. Would they have role models like Derek and Gunnar in their life? Would they tease each other with the obvious affection the Colton brothers shared?

"One hundred and forty over seventy-five?" Sawyer said tentatively taking off the stethoscope.

"Let's hope not," Gunnar mumbled.

"Sounds kinda high." Derek nudged his brother aside. "Let me check."

Derek pumped the cuff tight again and repeated the test. "More like one-ten over sixty five." He turned to Violet. "Which is very good." Then to Sawyer, whose face fell. "Don't sweat it. Just keep practicing." Derek gathered his supplies and stashed them in his medical bag. "We'll get out of your hair now. Thanks for letting Squirt scrub in."

Violet watched Sawyer roll his eyes at the nickname. "Any time."

Gunnar stood aside to let them through the door. "What are my orders, Doc?"

Derek flipped a hand casually. "Same as before, except she can get out of bed for short periods." He faced his patient. "Start putting weight on that leg, but don't overdo it."

"Got it."

Gunnar walked with his brothers to the front door, then returned long enough to tell her he was going to start dinner and ask if she had any preference what they ate.

"If there's any of that vegetable soup left, I'd love more of that."

He slapped the door frame lightly. "Coming right up."

When he disappeared into the kitchen, Violet sank deeper into her pillows. More than soup, she craved distraction, company. The brief visit from Sawyer and Derek had been a welcome relief to the tedium of lying in bed alone. She hated to demand any more of Gunnar's time and attention when she'd already turned his life upside down. But the empty hours gave her too much time to dwell on the attack, on where Mary Yoder might be and on how much she missed her boys. Tomorrow, she resolved, no matter how it taxed her, she would spend time with Hudson and Mason. Her boys needed her as much as she needed them.

Sophie sauntered into the room and hopped up on the bed with her.

"Hey, Soph. How ya been?" When Sophie

butted Violet's hand, demanding attention, Violet scratched her cat's cheek and stroked her silky fur. "You're mama's girl, aren't you?" Violet cooed to her cat, grateful for the feline's company. After a few minutes of loving, Sophie curled up against Violet's legs for a nap.

When Gunnar brought her soup, she invited him to eat with her and told him her decision. "I can spend an hour or so with the boys right before their naps. Once they're asleep, they won't know when I go back to bed. That way, they won't be as upset."

Gunnar eyed her silently for a moment. "As tempting as the offer of help is…are you sure you're up to it?"

"Derek said I should get up and about some."

"*Up and about* is sitting in the living room with me to watch TV. Time with your boys is more like hazardous duty or Olympic training."

She chuckled. "For you maybe. I can handle my boys."

He raised his hands in surrender. "Your call.

But if you're going to put in hard time tomorrow, I should let you rest."

He gathered their dishes and snapped off the bedside lamp as he headed for the door.

"Wait!" she cried, more plaintively than she'd intended, but she didn't want him to escape as he had the last several nights.

He paused at the door and sent her an expectant look. "Yeah?"

What did she say? The truth was she dreaded being alone with her thoughts again. She was just a little afraid of the bad dreams that lurked in the dark, but she didn't want him to feel sorry for her or decide she'd lost her marbles. "I—I've rested all day, and…"

"Want me to find you a magazine to read or something?"

"Oh. No…what I really want is… some company." She drew a deep breath and decided to lay out the truth. "I don't want to be alone. It's… well, a little unnerving. Would you stay?"

His shoulders tensed the slightest bit, and he

shifted his gaze away. Darn it, she should have known she'd put him on the spot.

After a beat of hesitation, he jerked a nod. "Yeah. Sure."

He took a seat and rubbed his hands on his thighs, clearly feeling awkward.

She searched mentally for a conversation opener, discarding several banal questions for the equally boring. "What were you watching on TV before Derek stopped by?"

"Basketball game. Score was real lopsided, though, so I'm not missing anything."

"Oh." *Great, Violet. How many "ohs" was that in the past two minutes? You are such riveting company.* "Wow," she muttered under her breath, "if the tabloids could see me now." Facing Gunnar more fully, she asked, "So…tell me about your family. Are there more Colton siblings out there?"

Gunnar raised his head and scrubbed a hand across his chin. "Nope. I think you've met all of us. Although, if not for 9/11, there'd probably be a few more."

She frowned. "What does 9/11 have to do with your family?"

"Our parents were killed in the attack."

She gasped. "Oh, my God. Gunnar, I'm so sorry!"

He gave a jerky nod of acknowledgment. "They ran a nonprofit organization out of the World Trade Center called Butterfly Hearts that helped inner-city kids. Most of us Colton siblings were in the system or the babies of teenage moms they worked with. If Mom and Dad hadn't died, I've no doubt they'd have adopted a few more kids before they were done."

"Wow. That's…so tragic. I… What happened to Butterfly Hearts?"

"It's still around. Run by a board of directors," he said matter-of-factly, with no outward show of emotion. "Funded through donations and a trust our parents established."

"I want to help. I want to contribute to Butterfly Hearts."

He arched an eyebrow. "Okay. I'm sure they'd

appreciate it. Derek can tell you where to send the check."

"You don't know?"

"Guess I should, but... having been out of country most of the past ten years, I gave my proxy on the board of directors to Derek. He's the one who's most involved. He handles my donations for me."

"Oh." Great. The "ohs" were back.

A crease pocked his brow, and he sighed heavily. "Guess now that I'm back CONUS, I should get more involved." His expression reflected a reluctance to do so, and she wondered about his hesitation but didn't ask.

"So Sawyer is, what, ten? Eleven?"

"Eleven," Gunnar supplied.

"Then he was just a baby when your parents died."

Gunnar nodded. "Yeah."

"I was fifteen, sitting in English class when our principal let us know what had happened. I cried and cried knowing kids somewhere had lost parents in the attack."

Violet's heart wrenched thinking of baby Sawyer growing up without his mother and father. She couldn't bear to think of Mason and Hudson growing up without her.

"Fifteen?" He looked and sounded stunned by that fact.

She lifted an eyebrow and drawled suspiciously, "Yeaaah. Why? How old were you?"

"Twenty-eight."

She did the math and goggled at him. "You're thirty-nine? You don't look that old."

"I don't feel that old—" he sent her a teasing scowl "—except when people tell me they were younger than Piper is now when 9/11 happened." He lowered his gaze and continued, "I was a personal trainer at a gym in Philly when the planes hit. Somehow that didn't seem worthy of the good work my parents had been doing. My answer was to join the army and go fight the people who'd taken my parents from me. I was in Afghanistan within three months. Stayed for eleven years."

His brows beaded, and his face darkened. "I

missed a lot with my family while I was gone. Piper and Sawyer barely know me." His voice trailed off, then he muttered darkly, "I'm the oldest. I should have been here to take care of the family, but I abandoned them to put my own ghosts to rest."

She narrowed a look of dismay on him. "Gunnar, you were fighting for your country! That is a noble and worthy choice. You sacrificed time with your family like so many other soldiers to defend our country. I respect that."

He lifted a dubious glance. "You wouldn't say that if you knew why I came home."

Violet's gut lurched, and she drew her eyebrows together. "What do you mean? I just assumed you came back as part of the draw down of troops. Did something happen? Were you forced out?"

"Naw. I left voluntarily. Officially an honorable discharge, but…" His jaw tightened, and he swiped a hand over his face. "Forget it. Can we talk about something else?"

Questions needled her, pinging about in her

brain and leaving her restless, but the stern expression he wore told her he was finished talking about whatever troubling thing had happened to end his military career. His secrets were none of her business, but she ached for him nonetheless.

Gunnar cleared his throat, rubbed his hands together. "So…tell me about your family. Are you originally from California?"

"Um…no." Violet took a moment to mentally shift gears. "Louisiana. A little town in the northern part of the state called Lagniappe. Two parents, both still alive and living in the same house I grew up in. A big brother and sister, both happily married. A dog and a cat. Very boring, dry subject. No skeletons. Don't believe any of the strange tales the tabloids like to print about my past. I wasn't raised by gypsies or part of a cult, and my father was a podiatrist, not a mobster."

He flashed a crooked grin. "Then you're not a mafia princess?"

She returned a teasing smile. "I only play one on TV."

"Do you see your family often?"

She turned her gaze to the covers bunched in her fists. "Not nearly often enough. The movie biz keeps me on the road a lot." After a beat, she added, "I miss them." To her horror, moisture pricked her eyes, and she blinked hard fighting it back. But one tear broke free, and when she drew a deep breath to regain her composure, a sniffle escaped.

Gunnar's head came up, and she felt his concerned gaze. "Violet?"

Damn it! She didn't want to cry in front of him. How pathetic was that? She raised a hand.

"I'm okay," she squeaked, only to have a fresh wave of tears rush to her eyes. Geez, what was wrong with her? She gritted her teeth and determinedly shoved down the ache in her throat. *Stop it, stop it, stop it!*

"I'm sorry." She hazarded a glance at Gunnar and met his deer in the headlights look. "I don't know what came over me."

He scoffed a laugh. "You don't? Really?"

She pulled her eyebrows together in query.

"Come on, Tink. You're in pain. You've been terrorized. You're worried about your Amish friend, and you got stuck in a cabin to recover with a grumpy, washed-up soldier." He shrugged. "Pick a reason."

She twitched a corner of her mouth in appreciation for his understanding, but none of his reasons resonated with her at the moment. She was silent for a moment, and the truth filtered to the forefront. "I just feel so…alone." She paused, then clarified, "Not just in the past couple days. I mean big picture. Since my husband died…before that even, I've felt—" she inhaled deeply and sorted through her thoughts "—being a public figure, it's hard to know who is being nice to you because of your star power and what you can do for them versus people you can trust, people who are really there for you. Even Adam betrayed me by cheating on me. While I was carrying his children, he was sleeping with other women. That much the tabloids got right." She groaned. "And how humiliating was it to have my husband's infidelity blasted in the media?"

Gunnar didn't say anything, and she realized the awkward spot she'd put him in. Why did she bring up Adam? She didn't want to get into Adam's infidelity now—or ever. She wanted to put it behind her and move forward.

"Geez, I'm sorry. I shouldn't be dumping this personal mess on you." She sniffled again and wiped her face with the back of her hand. "Forget I said anything."

He stood and crossed the room, headed for the door. Great. She'd run him off with her moping and complaining. She slid down in the bed, wanting to pull the covers over her head and hide for…oh, a few weeks would be good.

But instead of leaving, Gunnar picked up a box of Kleenex sitting on the dresser top, plucked out a couple as he crossed back to her and handed her the tissues.

Her heart thumped a beat, both in gratitude for his kindness and relief that he wasn't leaving her alone in the dark, gloomy room. As she blew her nose and wiped her eyes, Gunnar stretched out on the bed beside her. He opened one arm to her and tugged gently at her elbow with his other hand, coaxing her closer. "Come here."

Violet hesitated only a moment before scooting sideways to snuggle against his chest. He draped his arm around her shoulders and drew her closer still.

"Look, I know there's nothing I can say to make you feel better about the crap your husband put you through, so I won't even try. I respect you too much to feed you meaningless clichés."

"I don't expect you to—"

"But," Gunnar added, cutting her off, "the guy had to have had a screw loose somewhere to have cheated on a smart and beautiful wife and two great kids."

She opened her mouth to defend Adam, but the truth was Adam did have emotional issues and a chemical dependency. Not that either was an excuse for his infidelity, though.

"Of course, that's just my opinion, and you didn't ask so—" Gunnar shrugged "—next topic."

"Right." She shoved thoughts of Adam aside and rested her head on Gunnar's shoulder. The scents of laundry soap, vegetable soup and baby bath clung to him. He smelled like home and hearth and family. It was so ordinary, and yet he made the scents sexy.

Having Gunnar hold her helped quiet the restless loneliness and worries plaguing her yet also reenergized the hum of attraction she'd felt from the day he stormed up to her, demanding she move her bus from his driveway. Had that been less than a week ago? So much had happened in the past few days to change her view of him… and yet the underlying crackle of attraction was the same. Had maybe even grown stronger with all she was learning about him.

"Tell me more about the movie you're filming in town. What kind of scenes did they need our ranch for?"

She launched into a synopsis of the movie's plot and the shooting schedule, and soon they'd fallen into a comfortable exchange about new scripts she was considering, cute things the

twins had done this week and Gunnar's memories of growing up in Eden Falls.

"There's a place not far from here, a walking
trail that ends at a waterfall, that's a great place
for picnics." Gunnar tucked a wisp of her hair
behind her ear. "Maybe when your leg's feeling better I can take you and the boys up there.
I think they'd like it."

"I know the place you mean. The falls was one
of the first places the movie crew scouted when
we arrived. I think Mac plans to shoot the love
scene there."

Beside her, Gunnar grew still. She angled her
head and saw the muscles in his jaw pulsing as
he gritted his teeth.

"Do my love scenes *bother* you for some reason?" She studied the hard set of his mouth,
intrigued. She remembered his reaction to the
steamy film clip of her he'd found on the internet. He'd acted almost…jealous. The prospect
tantalized her.

His eyebrows dipped in consternation, but he

gave his head a stiff shake. "Why should they? None of my business."

"It just seemed like...you were upset. You tensed up." She smoothed a hand along the taut corded muscles of his arm, stroking her fingers to his fist to illustrate her point.

"Yeah, well..." He rolled his shoulders as if trying to loosen the tension stringing him tight, then sighed a gush of breath. "All right, yes. It bothers me."

The corner of her cheek tugged up, and she playfully goaded, "Why?"

He jerked his head toward her. "Why?" he echoed, incredulous. "I... Hell."

Suddenly he rolled to his side so that his wide shoulders and sculpted chest hovered over her. His hazel eyes lasered down at her with breath-stealing intensity, and the air between them sparked and crackled. A low, frustrated growl rumbled from his throat, and a heartbeat later, his mouth descended on hers.

Chapter 10

The first touch of his lips sent a paroxysm of sweet sensation coursing through her. Her eyes fluttered closed, and her brain short-circuited as his mouth directed hers with a seductive finesse.

She didn't think about what was happening. Gunnar's kiss felt too good to analyze whether it was a smart choice for her. She simply plowed her fingers into his tousled hair and melted in his arms. Violet savored the gentle suction of his kiss, the heady play of his tongue tracing her mouth, the tug of his teeth nibbling her bottom lip. When his hands stroked up under her pajama top, his calloused palms scraping lightly against her skin, she surrendered to the heat that clamored inside her.

This sensual escape was just what she needed, what she'd secretly craved all week while cooped up with the brawny and fiercely handsome ex-soldier. Gunnar covered her breast with his hand, gently flicking her nipple with his thumb, and thoughts of her attack, of delayed filming schedules and of her rambunctious twins fled her mind. Gunnar's mouth molded hers, demanding her full attention. His deft caresses left her head spinning and her body vibrating with a growing need. Clearly being mindful not to disturb her injured leg, he pressed her into the mattress, evidence of his own desire nudging her intimately. That skillful duality of arduousness and care was evident in other ways, as well. His commanding kiss left room for her to refuse him if she chose. His hands explored boldly, yet she'd never felt more protected or cherished.

Simply put, she wanted him. She promised herself not to second-guess the hasty decision to give herself over to something that was purely physical release, solely about chemistry and need and opportunity. No regrets. She knew instinctively that she could trust Gunnar, that she was completely safe with him. But ultimately, the choice became moot.

Gunnar raised his head, breaking their kiss and sucking in a lungful of air. "That's why."

She blinked, confused by his statement, and had to think back to the conversation that had preceded their intimacy. *Do my love scenes bother you...?*

"Oh," she said breathlessly, continuing her streak of brilliant responses for the evening.

He cradled her cheek with one hand and swiped at her lips with his thumb. "I'd have thought it was obvious. Hell, even Piper picked up on the fireworks between us the day we met."

She smiled up at him, loving the teasing glow that danced in his eyes and tugged at his mouth. "True. But sometimes a girl needs confirmation of her feelings, reassurance that what she feels is returned."

"Feelings confirmed, Tinkerbell." He smacked

a light kiss on her lips before rolling away and flopping back on the bed. Drawing a deep breath, he added, "But…"

She shifted toward him and laid her fingers over his mouth. "No buts needed. I think I know where you're going."

"You do?"

"Hmm, let's see…it's too soon. Too fast. We barely know each other. We're in totally different places in our lives. There's the kidnapping case, my kids, the movie I'm filming to complicate things. Different coasts. We want different things. Have different needs—"

"Wow," he said, lifting his eyebrows and raking his fingers through his hair. "I was just going to say we should wait until your leg had more time to heal."

"Oh."

Damn it. She really needed to work on her replies. She sounded like an airhead.

But Gunnar left her off balance, tongue-tied. He surprised her, confused her, intrigued her.

"But you're probably right about all that other stuff."

Did she detect a note of regret in his tone?

He reached for her and toyed gently with the shell of her ear, tugging on her lobe. "I know we're too different. And I'm not looking to start anything that would inevitably end. Probably end badly."

"Really?" Violet cocked her head, battling down the disappointment that squeezed her heart hearing him agree so readily with her assessment. "You think it would end badly?"

He hesitated before answering. "I wouldn't mean for it to. I'd never want to hurt you intentionally, but..." He flipped up his palm casually and sighed dramatically. "How could you help but fall for me and all my natural charm and animal magnetism? Giving all this up—" he gestured from his head to his feet "—would break your heart when it was over."

His cheek twitched, and she snorted a laugh. "Ri-i-ight. Gotcha."

When his grin brightened, the sight of his lopsided smile made her pulse trip. Maybe his comments weren't too far from the truth. Already she felt stirrings of an affection that went beyond the sexual sparks that arced between them. In the past few days, she'd seen another side of the surly oaf she'd pegged him for that first day.

Violet rested her hand lightly over his heart and murmured, "You know…I misjudged you."

His chest rumbled as he grunted an acknowledgment. "When?"

"The day we met…when the movie crew was here scouting the ranch for a location shoot." She tipped her head back so she could judge his reaction.

He twisted his mouth into a frown. "Well, that wasn't one of my better days. I can see why I didn't make a good impression."

"Hmm. You were a bit grumpy."

He half laughed, half grunted. "A bit?"

She grinned. "Okay, you were a lot grumpy." She paused as he met her gaze, then asked, "Why were you in such a bad mood? Do you really hate buses in your driveway that much, or had something else happened to set you off?"

He stacked his free arm behind his head, while the hand of the arm around her strummed her shoulder. For long seconds he said nothing, and she'd almost decided he planned to ignore her question, when he said, "I've had a lot of bad days recently. Grumpy seems to be my go-to mood lately. But that day—" he paused "—I'd… had an attack in town."

Violet frowned. "An attack? Of what? Like asthma?"

He shook his head. "More like a panic attack. Maybe a flashback."

She curled her fingers into his shirt and shifted again so she could better see his face. Tension drew his jaw tight, and his heart beat a little harder under her hand. She regretted the lost joviality, but something in his expression compelled her to pursue the topic. He seemed conversely reluctant and yet wanting to talk.

"Did this attack have anything to do with why you left Afghanistan?"

Again he lapsed into silence, but she didn't press him to answer.

Finally he spoke, his voice no more than a raspy whisper. "A suicide bomber."

Her gut clenched. Did she really want to hear the horrors he'd survived? How could she not listen when he'd done so much for her and her boys this week? When he'd sacrificed so much for their country? She held her breath.

"I don't know why it's gotten in my head the way it has. I saw plenty of action over ten years and five tours. I'd seen people die. Other soldiers, even children, women…"

Violet couldn't help herself. A tiny gasp of dismay escaped her lips and drew his attention.

His eyebrows pulled into a frown, and his mouth pressed into a taut line. "You probably don't want to hear this. It's not pretty."

Pushing up on her elbow, she cupped her hand against his stubble-covered cheek and drilled him with a hard gaze. "No, I want to hear. And more important, I think you need to talk about it. Go on."

His chest expanded as he inhaled deeply. His eyelids slid closed, and she felt the tremor that shimmied through him as he dredged up the dark memories that haunted him. "I was in the final weeks of my last tour, on patrol with a couple of buddies from my unit in a small marketplace just outside Kabul." His nostrils twitched as if he were back among the vendors, smelling the dusty earth, the meats and fruits for sale, the exhaust from passing vehicles.

"It had been a slow day. Nothing much happening, nothing on our radar, so to speak. I saw this little boy playing in the street, kinda pestering his mom while she worked her booth in the market. He reminded me of Sawyer a little. Mostly because he was about the same age Sawyer had been the last time I saw him while on furlough."

Gunnar's forehead wrinkled as he retrieved the events from that day, thousands of miles away. "He started kicking a hacky sack around and getting in his mom's way. He knew I was watching, though, so he kept kicking the hacky sack higher and doing tricks and spins to impress me. All his goofing around was really irritating his mom."

He tugged his mouth up at the corner in a brief sardonic grin. "But he was really good with the hacky sack, and so I was absorbed in watching him and egging him on with smiles and applause." Gunnar frowned then. Darkly. "I shouldn't have been so distracted. I shouldn't have encouraged him or he'd have obeyed his mother and maybe…"

A shudder raced through him, and a heavy dread flowed through Violet as she filled in the blanks with the snippets she knew. "The boy was killed by the suicide bomber, wasn't he?"

Gunnar's throat convulsed as he swallowed. He stared blankly at the ceiling and gave a short nod. "They all died. The boy. His mom." He paused. "My buddies."

"Oh, Gunnar," she breathed, devastated for him, for the grief and guilt and pain she saw in his eyes.

"I shouldn't have let him distract me. I wasn't doing my job, and—"

His ragged whisper faded, and she stroked his cheek. "And what?"

"I didn't see the bomber until it was too late. My buddies did, though. They charged toward the guy on the motorcycle, trying to stop him. They were just three seconds ahead of me, but... it put them in the blast zone. I had a concrete pillar between me and the explosion, so...I survived."

Survivor's guilt, Violet thought, remembering the research she'd done for a role a couple of years ago.

"Like I said, I'd seen the casualties of war before, so I don't know why this time felt so different...but it's stayed with me."

Violet couldn't breathe. She couldn't imagine watching friends die, seeing a child's life snuffed out. No wonder Gunnar was haunted. She stared numbly into near space, wishing she knew what to say to make everything better. He'd shared his darkest nightmare with her, and all she could do was shake and lie there like a log. All her brain could conjure were horrid images of what he'd described and asinine platitudes she was certain would do nothing but irritate him. But she had to say something. Her silence was deafening.

"Gunnar..." Her voice was a croak. She tried to swallow, but her mouth was dry.

"The day we met, I'd been in town with Piper and Sawyer. A guy with a backpack rode his motorcycle up onto the sidewalk, and I...freaked." He shook his head and grunted in disgust. "Piper thinks I'm nuts. And Sawyer..."

He scrubbed a hand over his face, his expression pure misery, and her heart broke for him.

"Hell. Who am I kidding? I shoved my kid sister to the ground behind an overturned coffee shop table to save her from an imaginary bomber. Maybe I have lost it. I have nightmares most nights and flashbacks during the day."

He turned his head to meet her gaze, and the turmoil in his eyes sliced her to the core.

"Damn, what was I thinking?" he growled and swung off the bed in one brusque motion. He plowed both hands through his hair and sucked in a shuddering breath. "I shouldn't have kissed you. The last thing you need is a screwed up vet like me in your life."

He stormed to the door, his thundering steps echoing through the dark room.

"Gunnar, wait!" Violet cried, desperate to do or say something to ease his suffering. But he disappeared into the hall, and she didn't see him again the rest of the night.

The nightmares were especially vivid that night.

With a gasp, Gunnar sat up in his bed, startling Violet's black cat from the foot of the mattress where she'd been curled in a ball sleeping. Bathed in sweat and shaking, Gunnar fought to calm his ragged pulse. Tonight it had been Violet in the marketplace, her boys playing at her feet. Piper and Sawyer had been sitting with him at a café when the suicide bomber sped down the street. His brother and sister had run to save the twins and had been caught in the fiery blast.

A sob of grief and guilt at the thought of losing his family, the twins...*Violet* caught in his throat. Tossing back the covers, he staggered to his bathroom and splashed his face with cold water. Gunnar stared into the mirror over the sink and barely recognized the face looking back at him: shadows under his eyes, stubble on his face, creases framing his mouth and eyes. He'd let himself go these past few months, and the stress of the memories that haunted him had taken its toll. No wonder Derek and Piper were worried about him. He looked...old.

You don't look that old.

He sighed, adding "age gap" to his list of the differences between him and Violet. Maybe the thirteen-year gap in their ages shouldn't matter, but on nights like tonight when his demons haunted him, he felt every one of his thirty-nine years...and more.

Derek's plea that he talk to a counselor replayed in his head.

Gunnar gritted his teeth. He'd told Violet the whole ugly incident—the boy with the hacky sack, his buddies' three-second lead, his complicity.

The horror in her eyes said what she hadn't. She pitied him. She saw the colossal mess his life was and couldn't run far enough fast enough.

Gunnar squeezed his eyes shut and clenched his teeth. He shouldn't have kissed her. No matter how tempting she'd looked or how warm she'd felt pressed against him, he shouldn't have opened that can of worms. Now he knew just how sweet she tasted and the nirvana he'd be missing when he couldn't hold her, kiss her… love her. Because he had no doubt he could fall in love with her. He was well on his way as it was.

By Friday, Violet had spent four and a half days cooped up in Gunnar's guest room, and she was getting stir crazy. When Gunnar came in to get her breakfast dishes and asked if he could do anything else for her, her reply was immediate and firm. "Yes. Get me out of here."

He stilled and frowned, his gaze assessing,

and she knew he was thinking about their kisses last night, his openness about his PTSD and his abrupt departure from her room. An unspoken tension hung in the room that she knew needed to be addressed—once she knew what to tell him.

"You want to go back to the movie set or to California or—?"

She shook her head. "Nothing that drastic. The front porch will do. Maybe the boys can play in your front yard, and I can get some fresh air. As great as you've been, taking care of me and my boys, letting me convalesce and invade your sanctuary…" She plowed her fingers through her short hair and blew out a deep breath. "I'm not used to being idle for so long. I'm tired of being in this bed, working crossword puzzles and playing Angry Birds on my phone. I need a change of scenery."

He folded his arms over his chest and regarded her with a thoughtful expression. "It's pretty cold outside."

"The boys have coats and hats, and I can take

a blanket." She glanced to the window where November sunshine streamed in. "C'mon. It's a beautiful day."

He flipped up a palm and stepped toward her bedside. "Derek didn't say you couldn't. Why not?" As she tossed back the covers, he handed her a bathrobe from the end of the bed, wrinkling his nose at the wrap. "This thing is covered in cat hair."

Violet grinned. "I know. What can I say? It's Romeo's favorite place to sleep, and I love having him and Sophie cuddle next to me."

His gaze darted to hers, and the heat in his eyes told her he was remembering how he'd been the one snuggled next to her last night. Her heart pattered, and for a moment, she forgot to breathe. She'd promised herself that their kiss had been a one-time thing, an impulsive act that she wouldn't beat herself up over but also wouldn't repeat. But, oh heavens, the man's kiss had teased her imagination through the long hours she'd spent with little else to do but dwell on how skillful his lips were.

When she hadn't been obsessing over his kiss, she'd mulled over what she could do or say to ease his grief and guilt over the bombing and concluded there was nothing she could do. Gunnar needed to talk to a professional counselor. He needed time to put the events in perspective and the guidance of someone who could help him cope with the traumatic events he'd witnessed. He needed the love and support of his family and friends, which he clearly had. For that much, she was thankful.

What he *didn't* need was the media circus and unrelenting spotlight the paparazzi would put on him if she were part of his life. Remembering this would help firm her resolve to fight the temptation to kiss him again. Besides, she'd already had a relationship with a man in a losing fight with personal demons, and she couldn't put herself or her children through that turmoil again. When she'd married Adam, she'd thought she could change him, save him. She'd been wrong, and she had the scars on her heart to prove it.

While she pulled on the bathrobe, Gunnar opened a cedar chest under the window and pulled out a patchwork quilt.

"Oh, wow," she gasped. "Gunnar, that's beautiful. Is it handmade?"

He unfolded it with a quick shake, revealing the intricate detail. "Probably. I bought it in town from an Amish crafts sale. Piper saw it and insisted it was perfect for the cabin. Frankly, I just think she likes spending my money."

"Speaking of money," she said, unsure how to raise a touchy subject, "I want to pay you for my time here. I know you spent a lot buying baby-proofing stuff and—"

"No." He shook his head and held up a hand. "No chance. I was happy to do it."

"Gunnar," she pressed, not wanting to make him uncomfortable but unwilling to be a financial burden on him either—not when she made ridiculously generous sums for her movies. "I know you're not working now, and I've heard how little the military pays…"

"Stop." His expression drilled her, but he

seemed more amused than irritated or embarrassed. "I don't need your money."

"But I heard you talking to Tate the other night, and I know he's hit you up to bankroll his investigation into the online sex ring…"

"You heard that, huh?" He twisted his mouth in consternation.

"I didn't mean to eavesdrop, but my door was open and—"

He waved a hand in dismissal. "Whatever. Just…don't mention it to anyone. I'd rather my part in funding the operation stay anonymous."

She nodded. "Of course. But with so many drains on your account, I can't in good conscience be another—"

"Violet, please." He chuckled awkwardly and scrubbed a hand over his face. "My finances are in good shape. Very good shape."

His embarrassed grin intrigued her. "Really? You're not just saying that to make me feel better?"

"Really. I invested in a few speculative stocks years ago that tripled in value before the 2008 downturn. Sensing things were about to slide, my broker sold the stocks near their peak value and waited out the market plunge. Then when Wall Street had bottomed out, he bought back those stocks and a couple other bargains, and I rode the wave back up."

She arched an eyebrow, impressed. "Mr. Buy Low, Sell High, eh?"

"Simple but true."

She bit her bottom lip and eyed him curiously. She was dying to ask how much he'd made but knew that was far too personal. Apparently, the question was etched in her face, though, because as he draped the quilt around her shoulders, he said flatly, "I'm a billionaire, Violet."

Her chin snapped up, and she jerked a stunned gaze to him. "I'm sorry, but was that a *B,* as in *billion?*"

"You heard right. I came home from Afghanistan to find out my investments had skyrocketed, and I have more money than I could ever spend. I'm still adjusting to the idea myself, so most of it is sitting in the bank waiting for the next worthy cause."

Violet was so startled that she didn't know which of the many questions buzzing through her to ask first. Instead, she glanced around his modest cabin and stammered, "But you…you don't…"

"Act rich?" He shrugged. "I don't want a big house to rattle around in by myself, and after being out of country for the past eleven years, I'd rather be near my family than traveling. While I decide what I *do* want to do with the rest of my life, I'm giving a lot of money to charities— mostly children's causes around the world. In honor of my parents." He rolled up his palm casually. "I bought Derek all sorts of medical equipment for his office and opened trust funds for Piper and Sawyer to use for college, but… that's about it. Underwriting Tate's undercover op is the least I can do for my brother, especially if it will help bring those Amish girls home."

Violet clutched the quilt closed at her throat and gaped at Gunnar. A fresh wave of respect for him flowed through her. How many times had she seen money go to her friends' and associates' heads? A windfall in Hollywood often got squandered on fast living and expensive baubles. Yet Gunnar used his money to help needy children and support his family. Layer by layer, she was peeling back fascinating new aspects of Gunnar's personality and ethics.

She blinked hard a few times to shake herself from the daze his revelation had put her in. "That's...fantastic, Gunnar. I'm speechless."

"Good. Let's leave it that way. I don't want anyone but those closest to me to know the truth, and I don't like to talk about it much. So...can you play it close to the vest?"

She nodded stiffly, wondering what it meant that he'd trusted her with his secret. But since he'd shared the truth about his lingering ghosts from the marketplace bombing with her, maybe he figured his bank balance was small beans on the confidentiality scale. Whatever his reason, she was no stranger to keeping private information quiet and respected his desire for secrecy.

She had little time to ponder the question further before he swept her into his arms, quilt and all, and headed to the front porch with her. Violet wrapped her arms around Gunnar's neck and clung tight, even though he held her securely. A giddy thrill chased through her as she nestled against his broad chest and felt the strong and steady thump of his heart against her own ribs. He hadn't shaved yet, and the shadow of beard darkening his jaw added to his rugged appeal. The morning was cool, as he'd said, but comfortable, and the scent of fallen leaves and rich earth perfumed the air. Violet inhaled deeply, savoring the fresh air, and caught a hint of mingled soap, coffee and man that surrounded Gunnar. The combination of pleasant scents was maddeningly sexy and, at the same time, relaxing to her.

He settled her in the one rocking chair on the porch, then stepped back, eyeing her. "That work?"

"Perfect. Except…there's no chair for you. You aren't going to leave me out here without company, are you?" She tipped her head and flashed a lighthearted grin, although his dark mood and abrupt departure last night still hovered at the edges of her thoughts. She waited, taking her cues from him. She wouldn't push him to talk about it if he didn't want to.

A car pulled up to the cabin, stalling any response he would have made. "That's Derek with your boys. I'll be right back."

She craned her neck to see around a natural stone pillar and smiled as she watched Derek and Gunnar get Mason and Hudson out of their car seats.

Mason spotted her immediately and wiggled to get free. "Mommy!"

Hudson's head came up, and he searched for what his brother had seen. When he saw her, he, too, struggled to get down, whimpering for her. Derek gave a wave from his car and called a greeting before climbing in the front seat and driving away.

Gunnar carried the twins to the porch, one under each arm like sacks of potatoes, as their legs pumped and their arms stretched out for her. "Mommy! Mommy!"

Her heart swelled with love. "Hi, guys! I've missed you! Come give me a kiss."

Gunnar set them down on the porch, and her twins ran to her. They threw themselves against her legs, pulled at the quilt to climb into her lap and babbled happily. Like excited puppies, they squirmed and giggled and clutched her neck. She hugged and kissed them one at a time, carefully holding their feet away from the wound on her injured leg...until Hudson decided Mason had been cuddled long enough and launched himself onto her lap, knocking into her wound.

"Yeowch!" she cried as pain slid through her.

Gunnar lunged forward and grabbed both toddlers off her in seconds. "Sorry. My bad. I shouldn't have let them climb on you."

"Don't be silly. Getting hugs from my babies is the best medicine there is. I'm fine."

"Just the same...let me see if I can distract them with some yard toys so you can relax." He carried the boys down to the yard and used his feet to pile up some leaves. He dug a couple of their toys out of the diaper bag but needn't have bothered. Mason and Hudson were fascinated by the crisp and colorful autumn leaves. They crunched, threw and rolled in the fallen foliage, laughing for all they were worth.

Gunnar returned to the porch, wearing a satisfied grin. "That's such a great sound, babies laughing."

Violet nodded her hearty agreement, glad to see Gunnar smiling after being so tense and guilt-ridden last night. "The best."

He turned to observe the twins for a minute and chuckled. "I've babysat those critters for three days now, and I'll be damned if I can tell them apart yet. They're carbon copies of each other."

Violet wrinkled her nose in disagreement. "Oh, not so. They're different in a lot of ways."

"All right," he said, closing the distance between them. "Enlighten me."

"Well, for starters, Hudson—"

Gunnar bent at the waist and scooped her into

his arms again, lifting her as easily as if she were one of the toddlers. Turning, he sat down in the rocking chair with Violet draped across him. With her bottom snuggled in his lap, his muscular arm across her back and her legs dangling comfortably over the arm of the rocking chair, she was cradled against his warm body and secure in his embrace. For a moment, the intimate position scattered her thoughts, and all she could do was stare up into his incredibly sexy hazel eyes, remembering the feel of his lips on hers and his hands on her skin.

"You were saying? Hudson…" he prompted.

"Oh…uh, right." She swallowed hard, trying to moisten her suddenly dry mouth. "Hudson loves nothing more than to explore new places. To climb and run and make noise. He's both fearless and fiercely protective of his brother."

Gunnar's expression said he was absorbing the information and processing it.

"Mason is the intellect. He figures out puzzles and games first. He likes to observe and absorb information. He remembers people and places, and he loves story time and snuggling. You may have noticed he saw me first when they got out of the car. He's more alert to things and people around him."

He lowered his brow a bit and nodded. "Okay."

"And Mason talked first and has a bigger vocabulary, while Hudson sets the pace and leads his brother into mischief."

Gunnar snorted. "Tell me about it. In three days, they've found more ways to make a mess than I thought possible."

"Hmm…sorry," she said and glanced to the yard where her boys were frolicking in the leaves. "I know my boys are a lot of work, and you're a good sport to pitch in with the babysitting."

He rubbed her arm and gave her a little squeeze. "Don't sweat it. I mean, what else is a hermit billionaire like me going to do all day?"

Billionaire. She still had a hard time reconciling that in her brain.

She shook her head in wonder, shifting her attention back to Hudson and Mason. "It's funny how twins can be so different in personality yet share such a close bond." She looked back up at Gunnar as she explained. "Have you noticed that if one of the boys gets hurt or upset, within seconds the other will sit down with him and join him in crying? And if they're separated for more than a minute or two, they search the room anxiously for the other and call each other?"

"Oh, yeah. I noticed the group cry thing on day one." He rolled his eyes. "So…how do you tell them apart physically? They look exactly the same."

She grinned. "There are subtle differences. Mason has a mole on his neck. Hudson's face is rounder, and he has a cowlick over his right eye."

Resting her head on Gunnar's shoulder as she watched the boys play felt as natural as breathing, and Violet shoved aside the voice in her head that wanted to analyze why. She tipped her head back slightly to see his face, and without thinking about it, she raised a hand to his stubble-dusted cheek. His skin was warm, a pleasant contrast to the cold air, and when she smoothed her hand along his jaw, the scratchy feel of his stubbly beard sent a tingle through her.

The muscles in his cheek tensed under her fingers as he clenched his teeth, and his grip on her tightened. "I'm sorry…about last night."

She sighed and turned his chin so she could look into his eyes. "I'm not."

Chapter 11

"Violet—" Gunnar said with a pucker in his brow.

"No, let me talk." A cool November breeze ruffled his hair and raised chill bumps on her arms. She clasped the blanket tighter around her and forged on. This conversation was too important to let him dismiss her concerns. "I don't regret kissing you because you're an excellent kisser and it was what I wanted, too. I still want to kiss you—"

"Vi—"

She covered his mouth with her fingers when he tried to interrupt. "But I know, for all the reasons we talked about last night, that starting a physical relationship with you is not in either of our best interests."

His dark eyebrows drew together, and he gave a quick nod of agreement.

"Pity that it is," she added, and his cheek twitched in a half grin.

"As far as what you told me about what happened in Kabul…and in town with Piper and Sawyer—"

Sighing, he pulled his chin free of her grasp and turned with a dark expression to stare at the yard where her boys were playing.

"I'm here if you want to talk," she continued, despite his distancing gesture.

"I don't. I shouldn't have mentioned it."

"You're wrong. The kind of grief and blame and regret you're dealing with will eat you alive if you don't get help."

"Violet, I *can't* talk about it." The ridges and planes of his face hardened, and her gut knotted with sympathetic pain. "You saw how telling you affected me last night. It hurts too much."

She gripped his hand between hers and clung to it. "I know it hurts, but the only way to put the pain behind you is to wade through it. Holding it at arms' length, shoving it on a shelf in some closet and trying to pretend it's not there leaves the possibility of it falling off the shelf and giving you a concussion some day when you go in the closet for wrapping paper."

Gunnar said nothing, then a beat later he furrowed his brow and shot her a puzzled look. "Wrapping paper?"

She stroked his cheek and brushed a soft kiss on his stubble. "Oh, so you were listening. Good. You know what I mean. It *will* be hard to talk about, but it's the best way to heal."

He glanced away again, his expression closed and dismissive. Violet took a deep breath and gave her argument one last shot. She knew she couldn't make him do anything he didn't want to, but he meant enough to her that she had to give convincing him her best effort. After that, his recovery was up to him. "I know that you guys, especially you warrior types, think you're conceding defeat or showing some kind of weakness if you admit you're struggling with something painful or emotional. But you're human, and you're not immune to feelings. Asking for help, getting counseling shows courage and strength, not weakness. You aren't meant to go through this alone."

Beneath her, Gunnar's leg jostled as he bounced his heel in agitation.

Fine. Enough. She'd spoken her mind. Pressing her hand over his heart, she whispered, "At least think about what I've said. You deserve to be happy."

He continued staring across the yard, but he gave a small nod.

Her heart aching for him, Violet curled her fingers into his shirt and snuggled her head against his shoulder. "Has Derek mentioned how Rani's feeling? I hope she's better in time for Thanksgiving."

She felt Gunnar's muscles relax when she

changed topics, and she prayed something she'd said had gotten through to him.

Please God, let him get help. He's hurt long enough.

Violet shifted her weight on his lap restlessly, and Gunnar gritted his teeth. He added holding Violet on his lap to the long list of poor choices he'd made recently. Having her soft bottom snuggled intimately against his groin, the scent of her body lotion cuddled right under his nose and her hand resting on his chest were enough to make a priest break his celibacy vows. After hearing her enumerate all the reasons they were wrong for each other last night, he'd sworn to himself to keep his hands off her. And as she'd just so clearly pointed out, she thought he needed help. She didn't need to get tangled up with an ex-soldier who had so much garbage to deal with. Too complicated, she'd said last night. And sex would only complicate things more. As much as they both liked their kiss, pursuing the physical attraction between them was off the table.

So why had he planted himself on the front porch with her perched in his lap, her sweet-smelling body rubbing him in all the right ways? Clearly he did need his head examined.

She moved again, nestling deeper in the quilt and grinding her tush against his growing arousal. "Can you believe Thanksgiving is next week? Where does the time go?"

"Yeah," he grunted. "Hard to believe." Gunnar tightened his hands into fists, fighting the urge to ravage Violet right there on his front porch. He cleared his throat and tried to redirect his thoughts. "By the way, Emma wanted me to ask you and the boys to join us for—" Gunnar paused when he noticed Mason staring at something in the woods "—Thanksgiving dinner."

He shifted his gaze to study the line of trees wondering what had caught the boy's attention. A bird? An animal?

"We'd love to. Tell her thank you. Or I will. I can call her…"

A light flashed in the brush about one hundred yards away from where the boys played. Gunnar tensed and narrowed his gaze, trying to decipher what he'd seen.

"Gunnar, what is it?" Violet asked.

The flicker of light came again, a reflection of sunlight on metal. A gun?

His adrenaline spiked, and not wasting time with questions, he lunged from the chair.

"Get down!" He twisted his body to put himself between Violet and the gun.

She gasped as he dropped to the porch with her, covering her with his body. She gave a small cry of pain when he crushed her under his weight. "Wh-what is it?"

He raised his head to search the wood for another flash—from a muzzle—and his eye snagged on the twins, sitting like ducks on a pond, vulnerable, exposed.

Hell! He had to get to them. But to do so would leave Violet unprotected. And she was, no doubt, the target. Because she could identify the Amish girls' kidnappers.

No time to debate.

"Get inside! Even if you have to crawl," he barked.

"But my boys—!"

"Go!" he shouted and scrambled off the porch toward the twins. As he ran stumbling down the steps to grab the kids, the trees rustled. In the woods, a dark-clad figure took off running.

Acting on instinct, prodded by the fury that some punk would dare to trespass on his land and threaten Violet and her boys, Gunnar gave chase. He raced toward the woods, slapping branches out of his face as he plunged into the line of trees. His gaze swung back and forth, searching for the man he'd seen. He glimpsed a gray coat retreating into the woods and charged after it. Pounding through the dense foliage and underbrush, Gunnar ignored the clawing vines and grabbing branches. His focus, his mission was clear.

Every step brought him closer to the intruder. The man struggled through the undergrowth, burdened with a large bag and dragging a piece of equipment with him. A tripod?

Pouring on every ounce of anger and protective energy, Gunnar closed the gap between them and caught the back of the man's coat. With a vicious tug, he brought the thug to a stumbling stop and threw him to the ground.

"You son of a bitch!" Gunnar panted, dropping to his knees beside his quarry and seizing the man's collar in a choking grasp. Gunnar reared his arm back, his hand balled in a fist.

The man raised both arms to protect his face. "No, stop! I'm leaving! I—"

Shaking with unspent adrenaline, Gunnar kept his fist drawn back, ready to pummel the man within an inch of his life. "Give me one reason why I shouldn't bust your chops?"

"Take it easy! I won't use the pictures. I swear!" the guy sniveled.

"Pictures?" The word cut through the red haze of Gunnar's fury. He looked at the equipment the guy had been hauling with him and frowned. The tripod had a camera attached to it, not a rifle. Knowing that the man had been shooting pictures rather than bullets should have been a relief, but disgust for the man's invasion of Violet's privacy snaked through Gunnar's veins. Releasing the man, he snatched up the tripod and swung it like a baseball bat at the nearest tree.

"No!" the photographer shouted as the camera smashed into small pieces.

To be sure the guy couldn't use any of the pictures he'd snapped, Gunnar picked up the battered camera, pried out the memory card, and shoved it in his pocket.

"That was a two thousand dollar camera!"

Turning back to the intruder, he hauled him to his feet and slammed him against a wide tree trunk. "You're lucky I don't do the same to your head."

He glowered at the jerk, and the guy's face paled.

"Who are you?"

"I'm a fr-freelance photographer."

Gunnar scowled and grated, "Obviously. What's your *name?*"

"What's it to you?" The guy must have had a death wish.

Gunnar tightened his hold on the man's collar so that the creep struggled to breathe. "What's your name?" he repeated through gritted teeth.

"Frank Greeley," he rasped.

Given a response, Gunnar loosened his grip on Greeley's collar. "How did you know Violet was here?"

The photographer lifted his chin and set his jaw. "I have my ways."

Grinding his back teeth together, Gunnar jammed his nose in the other man's face. "How did you find her?"

Greeley winced. "I…I saw her leave the clinic. I—I'd parked across the street and…wrote down the license p-plate number of the Suburban. Had a buddy in the DMV run it."

Gunnar narrowed his eyes. "So you cased the ranch, spying on my family, until you saw her here at my cabin? Is that it?"

The photographer had the good sense not to answer.

"In all your digging for information, did you also learn that the owners of this ranch include an FBI agent, a Philadelphia cop and a retired Special Forces soldier?"

The man's Adam's apple bobbed. "What?"

Gunnar tugged on Greeley's shirt so that the guy's feet almost left the ground. "I know twenty-five ways to kill you without a weapon. Only half of them are instant. The rest would be quite painful."

The photographer curled his lip, posturing, even though his eyes were wide and his complexion drained of color. "Is that a threat?"

Gunnar snorted derisively. "You bet it is. Get off my land and stay off. If I see you within a mile of Violet and her boys or any of my family again, I'll finish what I started today. Got it?" When the guy didn't answer, Gunnar gave him a little shake. "Got it?"

Greeley gulped. "Yeah."

He let the photographer go, thrusting him away and taking a step back. His body still hummed with rage and tension, and he drew a few slow breaths, trying to calm his pulse as the photographer collected his bag and edged away. Gunnar flexed and balled his fists, itching to hit something. When the intrusive cameraman was a safe distance away, Gunnar released the knot of fury and frustration tangled in his gut. With a roar, he smacked his fist into a tree.

Pain ripped up his arm and ricocheted through his body. He'd probably broken his hand, but at least he hadn't shoved the photographer's nasal bone into his brain or snapped the guy's neck. If the intruder had been packing a weapon instead of a camera, if the man had harmed Violet or her twins in any way, Gunnar would have hurt the guy without regret. Nobody messed with his family.

Shaking to his core, Gunnar sucked in another cleansing breath. *His family?* Violet and her boys weren't his family. Why had he had such a strong visceral reaction, such a powerful compulsion to protect them when he'd seen the guy lurking in the woods?

Because you care about them. Because you want them to be your family. The answer that rolled through his head rattled him. He was getting too involved with Violet, and that wouldn't do.

His heart thumped hard and fast against his ribs. With a shudder, he sank to his knees and flexed his hand, testing it. Okay, maybe it wasn't broken, but it hurt like hell. Either way, he had to pull himself together before he went back to the cabin. Violet didn't need to know how close to the edge he was—not after last night. She was already nagging him to see a counselor.

He shut his eyes, trying to regulate his breathing, but the sights and sounds of war he'd been running from since coming back to Eden Falls lurked behind his closed eyes. His buddies' warning shouts, the concussion of the marketplace blast, the blank stares of the dead. And the lifeless little boy…

He shook his head viciously, trying to clear the disturbing image. He'd thought he was making progress in putting the bombing behind him. But babysitting Violet's boys this week had been a wrenching reminder of the innocence of children, the Afghan boy who'd died far too soon and his own failure to prevent the boy's death. If he hadn't been distracted that day, would that boy still be alive? If he'd noticed the bomber sooner, would he have been sent home in a casket like his friends from the Special Forces team had been?

Huffing out a harsh sigh, he climbed to his feet and made his way back through the woods to his cabin.

Violet was on the lawn with her boys gathered onto her lap. Her wide and anxious eyes clung to him as he approached. His frustration with his jitters, the presumptive photographer and the potential danger Violet was in coalesced inside him and honed in on the most convenient target. He narrowed a glare on Violet as he stomped back toward his cabin.

She blinked her doe eyes innocently at him. "Well? What happened? Who was it?"

"What the hell are you doing?" he snapped.

A tiny wrinkle dented the bridge of her nose. "Excuse me?"

"I told you to get inside!" he steamed. "You're a sitting duck out here!"

She scowled at him and pulled her boys closer to her chest. "I was trying to get them inside, but as wiggly and heavy as they are, that's not easy to do with a bum leg."

He dropped to a crouch in front of her, breathing hard, his back teeth grinding together. "I said *you* should get inside. Not them. *You're* the target."

Violet gaped at him as if he'd grown a second head, then hiccuped a laugh. "Leave my children alone and vulnerable? In what universe do you really think I'd *ever* do that? Even if I didn't suspect a sniper was in the area, which you clearly thought there was, I'd *never* leave my children in order to save myself."

"You could have been killed!" He knew the point she was making, but he wasn't feeling particularly rational at the moment. When he remembered the terror that had streaked though him when he'd spotted that flash of light in the woods and thought someone had her in their crosshairs, a chill sank to his marrow.

"I don't care!" she shouted back. "I'd step in front of a moving bus to protect my children!"

Hearing the tension and volume of his mother's voice, Mason's bottom lip trembled, and he loosed a plaintive wail. Hudson, who'd been happily crunching leaves in his hands, stopped and studied his brother for a moment before adding his voice to the complaint.

Gunnar inhaled deeply, his nostrils flaring, and fought to calm himself. His hands stayed clenched to keep them from shaking. He studied the two toddlers, whose eyes leaked fat crocodile tears as Violet stroked their unruly blond curls, and his heart tripped.

He knew he'd step in front of a bus to protect the boys, too. Over the past few days, he'd grown attached to the mischievous imps. They were every bit as defenseless and needing his protection as Violet.

But he was just one man. If danger found them, how could he protect both the boys *and* Violet?

The responsibility to keep both Violet and her kids safe sat heavily on him. He'd be devastated if something happened to one of the twins. He dragged a hand over his face and sank to the frozen ground stunned by his realization. He stared at the cherub faces, damp with tears, and a rush of emotion squeezed his chest. He cared about Violet's boys as much as he cared about—

Violet.

Hell. The truth bit him hard, and he struggled for a breath. He wouldn't have been so scared by the thought of something happening to Violet if he didn't care about her—deeply. This week he'd seen other sides of Violet the starlet—a hurting side he could relate to, a loving side his soul yearned for and an intelligent side he found engaging.

She cooed softly to her whimpering boys, stroking their backs and hugging them close. The affection on her face, in her eyes, burrowed to his core.

She raised a gaze to his that still glittered with a hint of consternation. "So…who was it? Did you catch them?"

He shook himself from the disturbing track of his thoughts. "Photographer. The flash I saw was from a camera, not a muzzle."

Her shoulders drooped, and her expression darkened with defeat and frustration. "Great. I could live with the tabloids printing a picture of me sitting on your lap and all the inevitable conjecture about who my new lover was—"

Just the reference to him as her lover made Gunnar's skin flash hot and a prickly tension coil inside him.

"—but I hate the idea that they got pictures of the boys. I've tried so hard to keep them out of the public eye."

Hudson grew bored with snuggling and wiggled free of his mother's grip. He grabbed up the leaves he'd been crunching and tried to shove them in his mouth.

"Oh, Hudson, no." Violet reached for him, trying to stop him.

"I got him." Gunnar scooped the toddler into his lap and swiped a finger in Hudson's mouth, cleaning out the leaves the toddler now realized weren't so delicious after all. "There won't be any pictures. Not from that guy."

He pulled the memory card from his pocket and held it out, but instead of the memory card, her attention zeroed in on his scraped knuckles.

"Your hand," she gasped, seizing his wrist and pulling his arm closer to examine his injuries. "You hit him?"

"Not him, a tree." Though his hand was sore, her touch as she gently sized up his injuries sent warmth sliding through him. "Wish it *had* been him, the son of a—" he censored himself, then shook his head "—but trees can't file assault charges, and something told me this guy would have loved an excuse to draw you and me both into a legal dispute."

She raised a concerned glance. "Your hand is swollen, and you should disinfect those bloody knuckles."

"I'll live." He pulled his hand back and gave his fingers another test stretch and curl.

"Just the same, I think you should let your brother take a look."

He gave her a dismissive grunt. "I'm fine."

She pressed her mouth into a taut line of disapproval. "At least let me clean and wrap the scrapes. I make a pretty good nurse when needed." She scooted Mason off her lap and struggled to stand. "Help me get the boys inside?"

"Yeah, sure." He hurried to wedge his shoulder under her armpit and hoist her to her feet. Rather than let her limp to the porch, he scooped her in his arms again and carried her to a recliner in the living room. Returning to the yard, he lifted a baby on each hip and toted them in, out of the chilly air.

"I'm sorry you had to deal with that guy," Violet said as she took Mason from him and chafed the boy's icy fingers between her palms. "Telephoto lenses are part and parcel for me, I'm afraid. As much as I hate them, I'm used to the idea that my life is on public display."

Gunnar pulled Hudson's coat off and warmed the baby's hands the way Violet warmed Mason's, then set him on the floor to play.

Acid gnawed his gut when he thought of Violet being harassed by photographers. "You shouldn't accept it. It's not right that your privacy is invaded, your life put on display. I could never live like…" He let his sentence trail off when he heard himself, and he lifted his gaze to hers. An unspoken regret and understanding filled her face.

His life and Violet's were on divergent paths. She was all about the her career, the public spotlight and glamour. He needed his private escape, his family and a simple, uncomplicated life.

"Then it's good you don't have to live with it," she said quietly. "But for me, being a public figure means dealing with the paparazzi." She set Mason on the floor and struggled to her feet, wincing in pain. When he surged forward, ready to help her, she waved him off. "No more carrying me. Derek wants me to walk on it."

He followed her as she limped to the kitchen and indulged her as she cleaned the scrapes on his knuckles and held an ice pack to his hand.

Mentally, Gunnar added *nurturing* to the growing list of attributes she was surprising him with. So far, Violet had busted every preconceived notion he had about Hollywood starlets.

Except her looks. Even in a bathrobe with no makeup and sleep-tousled hair she looked gorgeous.

Violet bit her plump bottom lip as she worked on his hand, and his brain teased him with memories of nibbling that lip himself only hours ago. A low growl of frustration with his unrelenting libido rumbled in his chest, and she glanced up at him through a fringe of dark brown eyelashes.

"Am I hurting you?" she asked, loosening her grip on his hand.

"No, I…was just thinking about…something."

He scowled at his lame response and tugged his hand free of hers. "I think I'll live. Thanks, Tink."

"You really should have your brother take a look, maybe x-ray it."

A loud squeal of excitement from the living room drew both of their glances toward the door.

"That sounds like trouble." She started limping for the living room, and he stopped her with a hand on her shoulder.

"I'll check on them. You go back to bed. You've taxed yourself enough for one day."

Violet woke at—she glanced at the glowing alarm clock—3:25 a.m. with a desperate need to use the bathroom. She tossed back the covers, shivering as the cool night air hit her, and considered, for about two seconds, calling Gunnar for help.

No. She could do it herself. She needed to strengthen her leg, and Gunnar needed his sleep. The boys had run him ragged today.

Clutching the post at the foot of the bed for support, Violet limped to the hall. She made it to the bathroom and was halfway back to the guest room, passing Gunnar's door when a noise stopped her in her tracks—a moan.

Holding the doorframe for support, she peeked around the door to Gunnar's king-size bed. His legs thrashed in the already tangled sheets and blanket, and he huffed fast, agitated breaths.

I have nightmares most nights and flashbacks during the day.

Her chest wrenched, though she was sure her pity was the last thing he wanted. Still, she couldn't in good conscience ignore his suffering and go back to bed as if she had seen nothing. Limping to his bed, she considered the wisdom of waking him while he was dreaming something dark and terrible. Would he lash out? Be disoriented?

Biting her lip, she started tugging his sheets free of his legs and smoothing out his covers. What else could she do? When one of the twins woke crying in the night, she sang to them as she rocked them back to sleep. But Gunnar was twice her size, so rocking him was out of the question. She thought of how he'd held her earlier on the porch, cradling her on his lap. She'd felt so safe and comfortable cuddled close to him...until he'd dumped her on the floor to run after the photographer.

He moaned softly again, his body jerking in reaction to whatever disturbing images played in his dream. Willing to try anything once, Violet began humming the first song that came to mind, a Christmas carol, and brushed his cheek with the back of her hand. For a minute or two, nothing changed. He seemed as restless and uneasy as ever, but she persisted, watching until the furrows in his face eased and the rapid rise and fall of his chest slowed.

When his thrashing calmed, she glanced at the empty pillow beside him. Being in his arms had felt safe for her, so maybe, just maybe, feeling her presence would help him sleep more peacefully. It was worth a shot, she decided, and hobbled to the other side of the bed. She crawled between the covers, already warmed by his body heat, and scooted close to him. Laying her hand on his chest and her head on his shoulder, she settled in to sleep.

And woke him.

He roused with sharp intake of breath and hard twist of his torso to face her. "What the—?"

"It's me. Don't freak."

He scrubbed a hand on his face and blinked hard. "Violet?"

"Yeah. I didn't mean to wake you. Sorry."

He sat up and scratched his bare chest, still clearly confused. "Is…something wrong?"

Her heart thumped uneasily. How would he react to her gesture? He was pretty touchy about his PTSD. "Um…you were having a nightmare. I heard you as I passed your room on the way to the bathroom."

In the faint glow of his alarm clock, she saw him frown.

She rushed on, "I thought I could help calm you, the way I do the boys when they—"

His frown deepened, and she realized how that

sounded. He would not want to be babied or cod-
dled. She gnawed her lip and sighed. "I thought
you might sleep better if I…kept you company.
I—" Violet shook her head "—never mind. I'll
go now…"

She rolled away and shoved the covers aside.

"Wait." His hand clamped on her wrist. "Did
I say you had to go?"

"I just—"

He tugged lightly on her arm and rolled to his
back. "Stay if you want to. I don't mind."

She considered it for a moment. "Do you want
me to stay?"

He shot her a wry look. "I'm a guy. It's like an
unwritten guy rule to never kick a pretty woman
out of your bed."

She held up a hand. "This isn't about sex, Gunnar. I just thought you might sleep more rest-
fully if I stayed."

With his fingers, he made a cross mark over
his heart. "Not about sex. I promise."

Nodding, she scooted back against him, and

he wrapped an arm around her waist. "Good night, Gunnar."

"Night, Tink."

But for long minutes after that, she lay awake, listening to him breathe, trying to ignore the shivery sensation of her breasts nestled against his muscled frame. This morning she'd said nothing to him about his obvious erection pressing into her bottom while they sat on the porch. The night before, simply lying next to each other had led to heated kisses and nearly making love. It seemed the two of them couldn't just *be* close to each other and not have it turn sexual. Their physical chemistry ran too hot.

But she was determined to keep her end of their deal. The arrangement was not about sex. She honestly wanted to help Gunnar get a good night's sleep if she could.

When his chest lifted and fell in an even, deep breathing pattern, she peeked up at his square jaw and the unfair fringe of dark eyelashes closed in slumber. He looked so handsome, so sexy...*so peaceful*. She grinned. *Score.*

Satisfied, she nestled her cheek against him and closed her eyes in search of sleep.

The next day was a Saturday, and Piper called Gunnar's cell phone bright and early, waking them both and asking Gunnar if she could speak to Violet.

"Um…sure," he growled sleepily, then paused before handing the phone to his bed mate. He didn't want his teenage sister knowing he'd slept with Violet. When she held her hand out for the phone, he held up a finger silently, waited another few seconds, then passed the cell phone to her. "It's Piper."

Violet sat up in the bed. "Piper, is everything okay with the twins?"

"Oh, yeah. They're fine. I just wanted to see if it would be okay for us to take them to the zoo in Philly today. Tate has something he needs to do up there, and Sawyer and I thought it'd be fun to show the twins the animals and stuff."

"Would Tate be at the zoo with you?" she asked, her gaze following Gunnar as he slid out of bed and pulled on a pair of blue jeans over his boxer shorts.

Hearing their voices, Sophie pranced in and rubbed against Gunnar's legs as she demanded her breakfast.

"No, Tate's got something to do with work. But our nanny is going. You met Julia, right?" Piper said.

"Did I?" Violet asked, distracted by Gunnar's chest as he pulled a long-sleeved T-shirt over his head. "I was kinda out of it when I was at the main house before coming up here. But if she's going with you, then…I think it's okay. Be sure they wear mittens, and don't let Hudson stand up in the stroller. He likes to do that, but it's not safe."

"Got it. Wear mittens and keep butts in the stroller seat. So…how are you feeling?"

"Better, thanks. Much stronger since Monday." Violet raked fingers through her hair, knowing she had to have bedhead worse than her boys ever had. "Hey, when I checked in with Rani last night, she told me about your good news. Congrats on the awesome SAT score!"

"Oh, yeah. I'm petty stoked. It's a relief to have that behind me. Derek wants me to take it again and try for a perfect score, but I don't know…"

"Why not? It's not like they can take away this score."

"True."

"Well, congrats anyway. And thank you, Piper, for helping out with my kids. Your family has been a godsend, taking us in, babysitting the boys…"

"No problem. Hudson and Mason are soooo cute!" Piper said. "Oh…Tate says we'll be in Philly until midafternoon, back to the ranch by oh-dark-thirty. Okay?"

Violet grinned. "Have fun."

She thumbed the disconnect key and flopped back in the bed, already missing the boys. Then another thought occurred to her. If the twins were with Piper and Sawyer at the zoo, that left her alone all day with Gunnar. She smiled to herself. She could deal with that.

Chapter 12

"Where are we going?" Violet asked later that afternoon as she and Gunnar drove down the long ranch drive from his cabin to the rural highway into town.

"You'll see," he replied with a lopsided grin.

After a late breakfast of pancakes and bacon, which Violet had insisted on helping prepare, she and Gunnar had sat cuddled close to each other on his sofa to watch a recently released action movie. Gunnar had provided commentary on which parts of the military action the moviemakers had gotten wrong, while Violet contributed her behind-the-scenes knowledge of moviemaking magic and her personal experiences with various actors and stuntmen.

When she found his chess set in a closet, she challenged him to a match—and beat him best two of three. She had doubts his full attention was on the game, however, when he made an obviously bad move that gave her the win in their last round. She had more confirmation of this when he suggested they get out of the cabin and take a drive.

"It's too nice outside to stay cooped up," he said, parting the blinds on his front window to peer out. "I know you've got cabin fever. Let's bust this joint."

After packing a wine tote with a bottle of red and two glasses, he'd helped her hobble out to a Porsche Boxster he kept parked behind the cabin, and they were off.

"Nice ride," she said smoothing a hand over the leather seat.

"My one splurge when I found out how much my investments had made."

She studied his large hands as he smoothly

shifted gears. He looked incredibly sexy behind the wheel of the sports car and a dark pair of stylish sunglasses. Her fingers itched to thread through his thick rumpled hair, and she had to sit on her hands to stop herself from touching him.

He cut a quick glance toward her before pulling out on the highway. "I don't drive it too often, 'cause the SUV's more practical when I have Piper and Sawyer with me. And I generally don't go anywhere that doesn't involve taking the kids somewhere."

"I gave up a MINI Cooper for a minivan when the twins were born and don't regret it one bit. But this—" she leaned back in the seat and sighed "—this is nice. You'd be right at home on the streets of Hollywood."

He pulled his dark eyebrows together and grunted. "No. The car might be Hollywood, but this part of the country, the family ranch is where I feel at home. I'm a small-town boy at heart."

"Mmm," she hummed in acknowledgment, a pluck of disappointment tugging her chest.

All day she'd been cataloging the ways she and Gunnar were alike and how they were different. So far the differences were winning. That fact shouldn't have bothered her as much as it did. It wasn't as if they were in a relationship. They'd only known each other a week, and she'd be moving out soon. Her leg was healing well, and her strength was coming back thanks to Gunnar's TLC.

But their differences did bother her—especially the differences in their lifestyles. Gunnar was right. He'd probably hate the hustle and bustle of Southern California.

"What about you? Do you like living in Hollywood?"

His question drew her out of her thoughts but mirrored them so closely that her heart gave an optimistic leap, as if to say, "See you're on the same wavelength. That counts for something."

"Oh, well…" She twisted her mouth as she considered her answer. "L.A. took some getting used to, but I've built a life there, and…yeah, I like it. You don't have to get caught up in the

Hollywood hype to love the weather, the opportunities, the energy of the city." She smiled wistfully. "It's great…when I'm there. More and more, I'm on the road, making movies, promoting my movies, attending film festivals and award shows and—"

She stopped and sighed, reminded of the upcoming award show season. She rubbed her leg and wondered aloud, "Think my leg will be healed enough by the SAG Awards in January that I won't be limping? It's hard enough to walk in a tight dress and stilettos."

"Don't know about the limp, but…you in a tight dress and high heels?" He glanced at her with an unmasked heat in his eyes. "That I'd love to see in person."

She returned a grin and gave in to the urge to finger his hair. "Maybe you could. I need a date, and I bet you would rock a tux."

He shot her a startled, wide-eyed look. "Me?"

She laughed, warming to the idea. "Sure. I'd be the envy of the town on the arm of a sexy mystery man." She shifted on the bucket seat to face him more fully. "What do you say, handsome? Want to be my escort on the red carpet?"

His mouth opened and closed like a beached fish's. "I, uh…seriously?"

"You don't have to answer now. It was just an idea. I don't have anyone else in mind, and I don't want to go solo." She forced a grin when he angled a worried look at her. Gunnar's hesitation didn't really surprise her, yet it still hurt more than it should.

"I'm flattered, of course, but…"

When he floundered again, she waved a hand at him. "Never mind. Forget I asked. It was a crazy idea."

Her shoulders drooped, and her excitement flagged as she turned her attention to the rolling hills and stretches of rich farmland out her window. For a moment, imagining Gunnar in her life had been a thrilling proposition. But too soon, reality burst the bubble of that fantasy, and she was back to the conclusion that had nagged her all day. No matter how much she enjoyed Gunnar's company, no matter how attracted she was to his sexy body and ruggedly handsome face, no matter how wonderful he was with her boys, he didn't fit in her world.

He put a warm hand on her knee and squeezed. "I didn't say no. You just caught me off guard, Tink. Can I think about it and get back to you?"

She twitched a smile for him. "Sure."

But she wouldn't hold her breath.

That night, Violet stared through the darkness of the guest room at the ceiling, a smile on her lips as she reflected on the day with Gunnar. He'd been sweet and thoughtful, a good conversationalist and welcome distraction from the nagging concerns from the past week.

She'd just closed her eyes in search of sleep when she sensed a presence in the room. Turning her head, she peered through the darkness to find Gunnar, his shoulder braced against the door frame. "Is something wrong?"

"No," he replied quietly, "but I couldn't sleep, and…I heard you tossing and turning, so…I thought maybe you'd like some company? We could talk or—"

"Sure." She patted the other side of her bed. "Come on in."

The tentative way he asked touched her, but the uncertainty in his voice didn't fool her. She knew exactly what he wanted, what he needed… what would help him get through the night without the nightmares that tormented him.

He settled in beside her, folding one arm behind his head, and she scooted over next to him, savoring the heat of his body on the cold night.

"So…what do you hear from the movie set? I guess your absence has put them behind schedule, huh?"

"A bit. But they're shooting scenes I'm not in."

"That's good. What, um…do you think—"

"Gunnar?" she said, touching his chin.

"Yeah?"

"Good night." She pressed a kiss to his cheek and snuggled down to sleep. Next to her, his body relaxed as if relieved to not have to keep up his pretense.

"Good night, Tink," he whispered, the nickname she'd once hated now spoken in a tone full of warmth and affection. Soon he was snoring softly, the sound of his deep, even breathing lulling her to sleep.

Sharing a bed became a habit over the next few nights, an unspoken agreement, an arrangement that afforded Gunnar a better night's sleep and gave Violet the sense of security and distraction from her worries that she craved…while also revving her attraction to Gunnar to a fever pitch.

Nothing like a promise that the arrangement would not involve sex to focus her thoughts on stripping Gunnar to his boxers and sating the fire in her belly. By Wednesday night, Violet's skin felt too tight, her nerves crackled and her blood hummed with longing. She shifted restlessly beside Gunnar. Even the crisp, cool sheets against her skin taunted her and made her edgy, more needy. She flopped onto her back and tried to avoid touching the warm body and soft cotton pajama pants next to her, tried to ignore the woodsy scent that clung to him. To no avail.

A frustrated groan escaped.

"You okay?" Gunnar asked, and when he laid a hand on her arm, she nearly came out of her skin.

"No," she said, surrendering to the truth. "I'm not okay."

"You need some more ibuprofen or—?"

"No. That's not…" She sighed heavily and rolled onto her side, facing him, curling her fingers into the muscles of his shoulder. "I need you, Gunnar. I'm not a good enough actress to lie over here and pretend I'm not about to burst into flames."

Beneath her hand, Gunnar's body tensed. "Wait…you said sex wasn't—"

"I know!" She pressed closer to him and tightened her grip, shaking with pent-up energy and need. "I thought I could keep our relationship platonic and uncomplicated, but…I can't ignore what I'm feeling anymore."

His body vibrated with leashed desire. "But your leg—"

"Let me worry about my leg. It's not an issue

for me." She plowed her fingers into his hair and pulled him closer, until her forehead bumped his and their breath mingled. "The hot, prickly feeling crawling through me and making me crazy is an issue."

"Violet…" His voice was a husky, warning growl.

"Gunnar, Piper called it right that first day. I've felt the heat between us, the sparks, the chemistry even when my leg was throbbing and my kids were crying and the worries of the world were crashing down around us." She smacked a kiss on his lips and stroked her toes down his calf. "And the thing is, with everything that's happened these past couple of weeks and the way you've responded…your patience with my boys, the way you've cared for me and protected us and opened up to me about the loss of your parents…"

Gunnar's eyes were wary but smoldering with a piercing intensity.

"Well—" her breath caught in her chest "—it all just makes me want you more. Sexual chemistry I can fight. But I don't want to fight sexual chemistry backed by respect and affection and gratitude and friendship and—"

His mouth caught hers in a breath-stealing kiss, cutting her off. When he broke the kiss, angling his head for better access, he muttered, "You talk too much, Tinkerbell."

She grinned as he seized her lips again and let her body, her hands, her kisses do the talking for her. She shimmied out of her sleep shirt and helped him lose his pajama pants, eager to feel his body against hers, skin to skin.

Despite telling him he needn't worry about her leg, he shifted carefully, avoiding her injured thigh, to position himself on top of her, between her legs, his hips nestled intimately against hers. Violet savored the heat and friction of his body on hers as he covered her with deep, open-mouthed kisses from her jaw, down her throat, to her breasts, her navel and back up to seal her lips with his. Every place he touched caught fire, her skin alive with crackling energy.

Her fingers explored the hard ridges and defined planes of his chest and abs while her tongue teased his earlobes and the hollow of his throat. He rewarded her efforts with guttural groans of satisfaction and more avid attention to those places on her that ached most for his touch. He tweaked her nipples lightly, and she gasped as sweet sensation shot straight to her core. He sucked one peaked breast into his mouth and caressed it with his tongue until her hips bucked off the bed, and she wrapped her legs around him with a moan. "Oh, Gunnar…"

Sliding one hand down the curve of her bottom, he reached between them to stroke her intimately. A tremor raced through her as the coil of desire inside her reached its limits. "Now, Gunnar. Please…"

When he didn't answer her plea, she reached for him. Her fingers closed around the proof of his desire, and his whole body jerked and stiffened. He released a hiss through his teeth, and he growled her name in a rasping pant.

She wiggled against him, the crisp hairs on his chest causing tantalizing tingles to spiral through her. "Please, Gunnar…"

"Condom," he grunted, levering away from her with obvious regret. His gaze locked on hers with smoky heat and ferocity. "Don't. Move."

He launched off the bed and stumbled to his dresser, where he yanked open a drawer and pillaged the contents with reckless abandon. He returned in seconds, ripping open a box and tearing into the foil packet with his teeth.

He climbed back onto the bed with her, his hands shaking as he covered himself, and he grumbled a curse when the condom wouldn't unroll fast enough. Chuckling, she knocked his hands out of the way, taking over the task before he ripped the thing in his haste. "Easy, soldier. I'm not going anywhere."

His head rocked back into the pillow, his neck arching, and another low groan rumbled from his chest as she settled the prophylactic in place. "You're killing me, Tink."

"Good." She stretched out on top of him and brushed a kissed over his lips. "That was the plan."

Wrapping her in a firm grip, he rolled her onto her back and settled between her legs in a heartbeat. Violet held her breath, anticipation zinging through her blood and making her body pulse with need. When he pushed inside her, her hands curled against his back, clutching, clinging. She arched into him, savoring the building tension but also feeling a growing tightness in her chest. The tender ache had nothing to do with her imminent climax and everything to do with the flood of emotions that crashed down on her, all centered around the generous, caring, protective warrior in her arms. With their bodies joined and her emotions raw, denying what she felt for Gunnar was useless. She was falling in love with him.

That thought followed her as she careened into the maelstrom of an earthshaking climax. Gunnar caught her sigh of pleasure with a deep and tender kiss. His own body shuddered, and his arms tightened around her as he joined her in release. The moment was perfect. Her body quivered in the aftermath of the best sex she'd ever had. Tears of affection and awe leaked from her eyelashes.

But Violet couldn't get past one intrusive, sobering thought. She and Gunnar were all wrong for each other.

Chapter 13

"Are you sure you're up for this?" Gunnar asked as they approached the front door of the main ranch house. "My family is great, but they can be kinda overwhelming all at one time."

Violet gave him a wry smile as she nodded. "I'm sure. After ten days of near isolation, I'm ready for a little overwhelming."

Overwhelming. The word fit what he was feeling that morning, in the wake of their lovemaking. As if by unspoken mutual agreement, neither of them had spoken that morning about what had happened in her bed last night. They'd shared a kiss or two as they fixed coffee and prepared to join his siblings for Thanksgiving festivities, but they'd both pulled back as their departure for the main house neared. They seemed of the same accord that they'd play it cool around his family, not give his siblings reason to speculate about the changes in their relationship—especially when he wasn't sure himself what, if anything, had changed. Maybe Violet saw their sex as just sex, just the convergence of opportunity, desire and consenting adults...even if he knew it had been nothing of the sort for him.

Something had happened to him last night that had rattled him to his marrow—something he couldn't explain, couldn't define, couldn't get out of his head.

"As restful as your cabin is," she was saying, and he forced his attention back to the topic at hand, "the quiet and solitude are not what I'm used to."

He forced a grin, even though the reminder of their differences stuck under his ribs like a fist. And maybe that was at the root of his sense of unbalance this morning. As great as the sex had been last night, he was crazy to think she'd ever be happy in a relationship with him. Forgetting who she was and what her normal life was like was too easy to do when he had her all to himself in the privacy of his cabin and snuggled against him in his bed. But his time with Violet was almost up. She'd healed well and could take care of herself now with minimal assistance. Tamping down the swelling knot of disappointment in his chest, he gave the door a cursory knock before opening it and standing back for Violet to go first.

"We're here," he called into the family room as they hung their coats on the hooks by the front door.

"In the kitchen!" Emma's voice rang from deeper inside the house.

Gunnar led Violet into the family room where Sawyer and Rani sat on the floor, playing with Mason and Hudson.

As usual, Mason saw Violet first and pushed to his feet. "Mommy!"

Violet bent at the waist to greet her toddler,

who charged toward her with a clumsy gait. Hudson, his attention called to Violet's presence by his brother's shout, also climbed to his feet to rush toward Violet. Gunnar stooped to intercept the pair, scooping them both up so that Violet wasn't unbalanced and knocked down. He propped the twins at his hips so she could hug and kiss them both.

"Thank you," she said, stroking Gunnar's cheek with her palm and flashing him a special smile for having anticipated her predicament.

"No problem."

Even though Piper and Sawyer were out of school on Thanksgiving break all week, Piper had brought the toddlers up to Gunnar's cabin for a few hours of play time with Violet each day. Despite her limited mobility, Violet had sat on the floor playing trains or blocks or reading books until he could see the exhaustion in her face. At that point, he mock-wrestled with the energetic boys and took them outside to run in the yard, wearing them out for their afternoon naps at the main ranch house.

Now Gunnar buzzed his lips against each of the boys cheeks, eliciting the giggles and squeals he'd grown so fond of in the past two weeks. Who'd have thunk it? A hardened war veteran like him growing so attached to a couple mop-headed imps like Violet's twins. "Happy turkey day, guys."

"Gobba gobba!" Mason said.

"That's right, sweetie." Violet kissed her son again. "A turkey says gobble gobble."

"Down!" Hudson whined.

When they squirmed, ready to play again, Gunnar set the twins on the floor, and they toddled back to the train set with Sawyer.

He motioned to the oversize couch. "Make yourself at home. I'm just going to stick my head in the kitchen to see if I'm needed."

Violet took his arm and pivoted toward the room from which tantalizing smells wafted. "Lead on. I want to say hello to Emma."

Gunnar helped Violet hobble into the kitchen, where they found Emma kneading dough, Piper mixing a bowl of batter and Tate carving a large turkey.

After various greetings and cheek kisses were exchanged, Gunnar studied the sticky dough on Emma's hands. "What are you doing? I thought I ordered premade rolls."

"You did. But I want to learn to make my own bread like Caleb's family does." She held up her dough covered fingers. "I'm thinking it needs more flour. It's not supposed to be sticky like this."

"Are Caleb and his girls coming today?" Gunnar asked.

Emma nodded nervously. "Yes. They'll be here in about an hour, so be on your best behavior."

"Aw, tomato-head," Tate said, his cheek dimpled with a grin, "where's the fun in that? Besides, Caleb should know what he's getting, marrying into our family."

Emma rolled her eyes and shook more flour on her dough.

"Give me a job. I want to help." Violet limped forward and peered in the bowl Piper was mixing.

"Shouldn't you be resting your leg?" Emma asked.

"Actually, Derek wants me to start using it some so the muscles don't get weak. It's healed well and barely hurts anymore. Besides, I can sit at the table and chop or mix something." She pulled out a chair and sat down at the trestle table in the adjoining breakfast nook. "Put me to work."

Emma nodded once. "All right then. Gunnar, grab those pecans. Violet can chop them up for the pie. And you can start peeling potatoes and carrots at the sink, then give them to Violet to cut up."

They joined the amiable flow of dinner preparation, laughing and teasing each other as they worked. Violet was a good sport about Piper's continued fan-girl behavior, going so far as to promise her tickets to her next movie premiere.

"OMG! Are you serious? I'd love that!" Piper rushed over to the table and hugged Violet. "That would be awesome!"

"Down, girl," Gunnar warned with a grin.

"I'm her bodyguard today, and I will take you down if you harass the lady."

Piper flipped him a saucy smirk. "I dare you."

Gunnar's eyebrows shot up, and he dropped the vegetable peeler in the sink. "You asked for it…"

Piper's eyes and grin both widened as he charged toward her, lowered a shoulder and carefully planted it in her stomach. She grappled as he lifted her, holding her legs and dangling her over his back in a fireman's hold.

Derek walked in the back door and deposited a casserole dish on the stove. "I see we've descended into chaos right on schedule."

"Derek, help!" Piper squawked.

"Gushy Sue was crowding the movie star," Tate explained.

Derek turned back to Gunnar with a deadpan, "Carry on."

"No!" Piper half laughed, half squealed as Gunnar lugged her to the living room and tossed her into the plush pillows of the sofa.

Violet's twins saw the horseplay and laughing

as an invitation to join in, and as he returned to the kitchen, the toddlers piled on top of Piper in a fit of giggles. Gunnar grinned to himself. Toddler wrestling had become one of his favorite ways to entertain the boys in the past few days. Not only did it wear them out before their naps, a boon in and of itself, but he enjoyed the horseplay, too. Though he kept his wrestling with the twins much tamer and gentler, the grappling matches reminded him of the rough and tumble games he used to play with their dad and later with Derek and Tate.

"Sounds like Mason and Hudson are having fun," Violet said.

"Boys will be boys." A pang of longing stabbed Gunnar as he picked up where he'd stopped peeling vegetables. After Violet left his cabin, who would the twins have to roughhouse with? Little boys needed a father figure, a role model… someone to play catch and teach them to throw a football. He cast a quick side glance to Violet, who was laughing with Emma about the massive quantity of pecans she'd chopped. The thought of another man at Violet's side, filling the role of husband and father, stirred an acid gnawing in his gut. The prospect of picking up a gossip magazine one day and seeing Violet pictured with some Hollywood pretty boy made him want to puke. She deserved more than a handsome face and A-list star power.

But what could he do about it? He'd already laid out a rather convincing argument why he couldn't make her happy, why his lifestyle and hers didn't mesh. Regardless of what happened last night between them, he couldn't burden her with all the messed up stuff from Afghanistan he was still dealing with all these months later.

I think you have PTSD, he heard Derek saying. *Talk to a counselor. They can help.*

Gunnar exhaled deeply. Wasn't seeing a shrink the same as admitting defeat? A sign of weakness? An admission that you had no control in your life?

Piper had called those excuses caveman thinking, but what did she know? She might have a genius IQ, but she was still a teenager. She hadn't seen the harsh realities of life he'd seen. He just needed more time to get the nightmares under control and push the memories down deep enough that he didn't have flashbacks like the one in town almost two weeks ago.

"Geez, such a serious face. What are you thinking so hard about?" Tate asked, bumping Gunnar out of the way so he could wash his hands. "Peeling potatoes is not rocket science."

Gunnar shook himself from his ruminations and shrugged. "Just deciding the best way to lace your potatoes with laxatives without ruining the rest for us."

Tate snorted. "You do and I can have you arrested for assault on an officer."

Gunnar flashed his brother an evil grin. "But it would be so worth it."

An hour later, the Colton clan and their company gathered around the massive dining room table and joined hands to say a prayer of thanks.

"Mr. Perfect, will you say the blessing?" Emma asked Derek.

Gunnar glanced down the assembled faces and

felt a catch in his chest. As much as he teased and ragged on his siblings, every one of them held a special place in his heart. Being with them this Thanksgiving, instead of settling for a short video chat from the front lines, meant the world to him.

The additional guests—Caleb Troyer and his daughters, who so clearly made Emma happier than she'd ever been; Rani Ogatani, the twins' nanny; Hudson and Mason, whose high chairs had been pulled up to the table between Violet and Rani—were all welcome additions. But Violet's presence at his family's table made his breath hitch. Having her seated next to him felt ordained, and when she slipped her cool fingers in his hand for the prayer, a warmth spread through him that had nothing to do with his sexual attraction to her and everything to do with the friendship and personal connection they'd shared the past ten days. Damn, but he didn't want her to leave!

He squeezed her hand tighter and focused on what Derek was praying.

"We thank you, Lord, for this food, for new friends and for the blessing of this family. We ask a special prayer of protection for Tate as he leaves tomorrow for his undercover assignment and ask that you will help the missing Amish girls be returned safely to their families."

"Amen to that," Emma said with feeling, starting a chorus of amens around the table. She and Caleb exchanged a poignant look.

"Ah-men!" Mason piped in, and everyone chuckled.

"Man!" Hudson echoed, not to be outdone by his brother.

Gunnar grinned at the two boys he'd spent so much time with over the past ten days, and warmth expanded in his chest. Violet's eyes sparkled as she ruffled Mason's blond curls, and something in her expression made his own reaction to the boys click. *Love.* The truth shook him to the core and shifted something basic in his perception of his private, quiet little world.

Through all the rascals' high jinks and mischief, he'd bonded with Violet's children. Their innocent laughter, their sleepy smiles after their naps and the spark in their eyes that spoke of blossoming intelligence had burrowed into his heart. In his new reality, peace and quiet included the sound of toddlers babbling with each other as they played. Privacy meant keeping two innocent boys out of the media spotlight. Peace of mind was found in knowing the ones he loved were safe, happy and close by.

His hands fisted in his lap as these revelations settled in his brain. He glanced at Violet and held his breath. Where did this new understanding of what he wanted fit in her plans, her goals and aspirations? He knew he wanted Violet and the boys in his life, but how could he make it work?

"Derek, you should have invited your nurse Amelia to eat with us. She's new in town, isn't she?" Emma said, lifting the bowl of peas and serving herself a scoop.

"I did invite her," Derek replied. "She declined."

"Why?" Sawyer asked.

Derek lifted one eyebrow as he faced his

brother. "I didn't press her for a reason, Squirt. That would have been rude."

Gunnar leaned close to Violet and whispered in her ear, "Can we talk after the meal? It's important."

She sent him a puzzled, somewhat worried glance but nodded.

His heart kicked. What would he say to Violet? *Give up your life and be a hermit with me. I may be haunted by nightmares of a bombing, but I only have panic attacks and flashbacks* some *of the time.*

"Maybe later you could take Amelia some of our leftovers," Piper suggested.

"Like Emma's rock bread?" Sawyer asked, tapping a slice of the overbaked loaf on the edge of his plate.

Emma scowled. "You don't have to eat it if you don't like it."

"Or if you don't want a broken tooth," Tate mumbled under his breath.

Emma redoubled her glower for Tate.

"Well, I, for one, am grateful to be included

in your family dinner." Violet shared a bright smile with the table.

"As are we," Caleb said.

"It's been a long time since I was part of a large family dinner like this," Violet said, "and I'd almost forgotten how much fun it was."

"Fun?" Piper asked skeptically.

"Just you wait," Violet returned. "You'll miss family gatherings when you're away at college."

Sawyer's face brightened. "Piper's leaving town for college?"

Piper elbowed her younger brother. "If you're lucky."

"Oh, no!" Rani said loudly and all eyes turned to her. She flashed an embarrassed grin as she started cleaning Hudson's hands. "Sorry. Didn't mean to be a distraction. I just realized Hudson was fingerpainting everything in reach with mashed potatoes, including his brother's hair."

Violet chuckled and pitched in, wiping food out of Mason's curls. "Poor Mason. Hudson, eat. Not play."

"I'm glad to see you are feeling better, Ms.

Chastain," Caleb said as he passed the platter of turkey to Emma. "You really gave us a scare the other day."

"Please, call me Violet. And I don't think I've ever thanked you for getting me to Derek's office so quickly. I think you saved my life."

The bite of sweet potatoes in Gunnar's mouth soured at the thought of losing Violet. He remembered how pale and fragile she'd looked when he'd first arrived at Derek's office—how vulnerable.

"I *know* he saved your life. You were bleeding profusely and—" Derek looked up from his plate and met Emma's silencing glare. He shifted his gaze to the wide-eyed horror worn by Piper and also Caleb's daughters. "Um…well, that's not table talk, but…you were very lucky."

The conversation turned to Sawyer's science project, building a working trebuchet, which was due before Christmas break, and Emma talked about all she was learning about Amish customs and beliefs.

"We are pleased with your progress," Caleb

said, giving Emma's hand a squeeze. "I know it is a big change for you, and your choice to embrace our way of life means a lot to me."

Gunnar glanced at Emma, studied the gleam of joy in her eyes. His sister was sacrificing a lot to be with the man she loved. She was changing her life to fit in Caleb's world.

Could he do the same to be with Violet? Could he ask Violet to give up her career to be with him? The coil of nerves in his stomach didn't bode well.

"Tate, are you at liberty to discuss your case?" Violet asked, hesitantly. "Did the sketch I helped with yield any tips?"

Tate and Emma exchanged a meaningful glance. "A few, but nothing that panned out. Our best hope is the undercover op I've been assigned."

Violet bit her lip and nodded forlornly. Gunnar knew from her expression she was thinking about Mary Yoder and blaming herself again for the girl's kidnapping. Under the table, he slid his hand to her knee and gave her a supportive squeeze. She raised a halfhearted smile of appreciation to him, then turned to wipe gravy off Mason's face.

"What are you gonna do undercover?" Sawyer asked Tate, his face alight with curiosity and enthusiasm. "Do you have a secret identity like in the movies? Will you wear a wire under your clothes and stuff?"

"Sorry, buddy." Tate aimed his fork at his little brother. "That's classified info."

"Hence the term *undercover,* doofus," Piper said sarcastically.

"Shut up, Amazon," Sawyer sniped.

Derek groaned loudly. "Both of you, give it a rest. It's Thanksgiving. Can't the arguing take a holiday?"

"But she—"

Gunnar cut Sawyer off with a wrong answer buzzer noise. "Was some part of 'give it a rest' not clear?"

Emma cleared her throat, then directed a smile at Violet. "So, Violet, if you think your leg is up to it, Piper and I would love to have you join us for some Black Friday shopping in town tomorrow. The local shops don't do the open-in-the-wee-hours bit, but they do have great sales."

Piper sat straighter, her face glowing. "Oh! Say yes. Say yes! Shopping with Violet Chastain. How cool would that be?" she asked of no one in particular.

"Doc?" Violet shot a questioning glance to Derek, who shrugged.

"If you feel up to it, I don't see why you can't."

Gunnar shifted uneasily and divided a look between Emma and Tate. "Is it safe? I thought the reason she was staying at the cabin was because you thought the men who'd attacked her might come after her to keep her quiet."

Emma stabbed a bite of turkey and waved her fork as she spoke. "She'll be with me. I'll keep an eye on her. And she's already given the police her statement and description of the perp, so his incentive is diminished." She stuck the turkey in her mouth and tugged a lopsided grin. "But if you're worried about her, big guy, you can come with us, too."

Gunnar didn't like the smirk in Emma's tone, and he wanted to go shopping with the women about as much as he wanted a hernia. But he wasn't ready to shirk his guard duty and felt compelled personally to keep Violet safe. "All right, I will."

Violet cut a side glace at him. "I hadn't said *I* was going yet."

"Please? It'll be fun," Piper said. "We've got some great clothing and shoe boutiques, and there are local crafts and one store with nothing but scented bath stuff."

Sawyer made a gagging noise, earning scowls from his siblings.

"Since I'm feeling better, I was going to move back to my room in town with the rest of the movie crew tomorrow," Rani said. "But I can keep the kids while you shop and then meet around lunchtime in town."

"All right," Violet said, "that sounds like a plan. I'm in!"

"Yes!" Piper said under her breath and pumped her fist.

Leaning back in his chair and rubbing his chin in a way Gunnar knew meant trouble, Derek said, "Seems to me, Violet, that if Rani's over the flu and you're on your feet, there's no reason for you to stay at Gunnar's anymore." His brother had drawn the same conclusion that had occurred to Gunnar in the past few minutes. "You could move down to the main house if you want."

"Or I could get a plainclothes officer to guard you," Tate offered, "if you're ready to move back to town yourself."

A flutter of panic stirred in Gunnar's gut as he glanced from one brother to the next and finally to Violet. Having Violet move out felt tantamount to losing her from his life completely and the end of the special friendship they'd developed.

Friendship? Hell. The past several days had been about way more than friendship. He'd lost a part of himself to her. He'd invested his heart and soul in her. He'd...fallen in love with her.

The dinner in his stomach lurched, and his lungs tightened.

He turned to Violet, working hard at keeping his expression impassive, hiding the desperation that clawed inside him. *Don't go. Don't ever leave me. I love you.*

"Violet?" he said, hearing the emotion that thickened his voice.

She wet her lips and swallowed hard. "They're right. I guess it's time that I move out."

Chapter 14

"You don't have to go."

Violet looked up from the suitcase she was packing before going to bed. Gunnar stood in the doorway of the guest room, wearing only his sleep pants and looking like he'd stepped off the pages of a catalog for chiseled masculine perfection. Desire rippled through her, remembering the feeling of that body next to hers, but she dragged her gaze away from his washboard abs and muscled shoulders and dropped her tube of toothpaste into the suitcase. "I've imposed long enough."

"You're not imposing. I…I want you here." He

pushed off the door frame and sat on the corner of the bed.

She offered him a grin. "You've been a great host and a tremendous help, but I have to leave sometime."

"Why?"

Violet chuckled as she gathered her brush, hairspray and makeup bag from the bed and shoved them in the travel case. "What do you mean, 'why?'"

Gunnar caught her hands, pulled her into the V of his legs and drilled her with a hazel gaze that shot straight to her core. "Violet, what if I told you I'd been thinking a lot about my future. And the one thing that I know for sure is that I want you in it."

Her body stilled, but her heartbeat kicked into high gear. "Gunnar...what are you saying?"

His grip tightened on her hands, and a muscle in his jaw jumped. "I'm saying...I love—"

Gunnar stopped abruptly and blinked as if taking a mental assessment. Violet's breath hung in her lungs. *Me. Say you love me,* she prayed.

No. Don't say you love me. It will only break my heart when I have to leave.

She saw no way around the fact that she had to leave. Even if their lives weren't different, Gunnar still had unresolved issues from the war that haunted him. She couldn't invest her life and her boys' with another man locked in turmoil with himself. Adam's demons had eventually killed him, and she couldn't go through that kind of personal drama and heartache again. She couldn't save Gunnar. He had to find the strength and courage to make the hard choices to save himself.

"I love…being with you," he said, his tone pitched low. "I love the sound of your laugh and the way you feel in my arms. I've slept better the past few nights than I have since before my first tour in Afghanistan."

She forced herself to swallow, wetting her dry throat. "I'm glad it hel—"

"I love having you to talk to in the morning," he added quickly, "and hearing about your family and your travels and your career…"

Violet pulled her hand from his and lowered herself onto the bed. Clearly, he wasn't going to make this easy for her. "Gunnar…"

"I want to build a life with you, Tink."

She didn't miss the fact that he hadn't mentioned her boys. "And the twins? We're a package deal, you know."

His expression said that was obvious. "Of course. I realized at lunch how much I'll miss having the boys around here if you leave." His cheek twitched in a sad grin. "I've grown to love the little scamps, Violet."

She sat up straighter, feeling a tug in her chest. "*Love* is a strong word, Gunnar."

Oh, Lord, but she wanted her boys to have the love of a father figure. But they deserved someone they could depend on to be there no matter what—even when things got tough. Adam had used drugs as an escape from the hard parts of parenting and marriage.

She smoothed her short hair behind her ear with trembling fingers. The importance of this conversation sat heavily on her chest. "It's easy to like babies when they're playing sweetly in a pile of autumn leaves or napping quietly. The real test comes when you're up all night with a baby who is crying and throwing up on you, or when they pitch a tantrum in front of your boss or disobey you for the hundredth time in a day about pulling the cat's fur. Parenting can be a frustrating, exhausting job. Sometimes as much as you *love* your children and would *die* for your children, you don't like them so much."

The lines around his mouth deepened. "Clearing IEDs from a roadway in Kandahar only to have new ones hidden on the same road within hours of you leaving is frustrating, exhausting work, too. But my team and I did it, day after day, because lives depended on it. Innocent civilian lives, as well as the lives of fellow soldiers I'd come to love like brothers."

Violet frowned. "You're comparing raising twin toddlers to warfare?"

He sighed. "Only because it's what I know. That was my life for the past eleven years." He dragged his hand through his rumpled hair, then turned up his palm. "My point is I'm not afraid of hard work or difficult circumstances. I care about Hudson and Mason, and I want to see them grow up, even if that means staying up all night when they're sick or endlessly mediating squabbles, like the ones Sawyer and Piper have, when they're older."

Violet fingered a loose thread on her travel bag. "They've taken to you, too. They trust you. But…"

But was that enough? Gunnar loved spending time with her and would miss the boys when they left. That wasn't enough to build a relationship on—especially a relationship destined to be as difficult as theirs would be. He loved *hearing* about all the crazy aspects of her film career, but living it was a whole different story. The public spotlight, the media scrutiny, the lack of privacy would be devastating for Gunnar. The barrage of the press and clamoring fans was stressful enough without adding his lingering issues dealing with his trauma in Afghanistan. Her life was not suited for someone like Gunnar.

"But what, Tink?" he prompted, reaching for her again. "You can't deny there's something real and meaningful happening between us. Last night proved that, Violet."

A knot lodged in her throat, and she couldn't speak. She knew there was more than sexual chemistry, more than friendship blossoming between them, too. But her growing feelings for Gunnar only made it harder to do the right thing.

"I'm asking you to be part of my life. You and the twins." He trapped her hand between his, and the strength and warmth of his grasp reminded her how safe she'd felt the past several days in his cabin, in his bed, in his arms…

Tears stung her eyes. She wanted desperately to stay with Gunnar and pretend the real world didn't exist, but her life was not a movie, not make-believe, and she had to face the truth. Her world and Gunnar's didn't mesh. She cared too deeply for him to put him through the turmoil of having his life dissected and put on public display. It was too much to ask of an average man, much less a man coping with PTSD. She had to think of her boys, had to protect her heart, had to put Gunnar's happiness first.

She opened her mouth, but no sound came out. Emotion choked her.

He brushed his fingers along her cheek, and a wistful smile ghosted across his lips. "I'm saying I love you, Tinkerbell. Stay with me."

Pain slashed through her chest, and wrenching away from his touch, she pushed to her feet, giving him her back while she fought for composure. Violet muffled a sob behind her hand and battled tears. Damn, this was hard!

"Violet?"

She shook her head and faced him slowly. "I can't, Gunnar. I can't stay with you."

A scowl furrowed his brow. "Why not?"

"I…I have commitments…my career."

"I'm not asking you to give up your career. I'll move to California—"

"No. I—" she squeezed her eyes shut for a

moment, and twin tears leaked from her lashes "—Gunnar, the truth is…there's no room in my life for you."

He jerked as if shot, his expression stunned, hurt.

"I care about you, Gunnar," she rushed to explain. "Truly I do. But you have to resolve your issues with the bombing in Afghanistan before I can even think about building a life with you."

His mouth hardened as he stood from the bed. "I'm too damaged for you? Is that it?"

"I didn't say that!" She swiped the moisture from her cheeks. "I know this hurts you, and I'm sorry. But I've had a husband who ignored the truth about his personal demons, and his problems destroyed our marriage long before they killed him. If I learned nothing from the crap Adam put me through, I learned that I can't save someone with an anchor around their neck. We'll both drown."

Gunnar aimed a finger at her, his expression impassioned, pleading. "I would *never* hurt you or your children, Violet. You know I wouldn't."

"I know you wouldn't mean to. But just seeing you suffer through your nightmares hurts me." She dared to step closer to him and stroke the tense muscles in his jaw. "You don't have to carry this guilt and grief that's tormenting you. Talk to a professional. Do whatever therapy or counseling they advise for as long as it takes."

"I'm so sick of people telling me I need a shrink," he grumbled.

He clenched his teeth and dropped his gaze to the floor. His hurt was etched in the lines bracketing his mouth and eyes. His pain rolled off him in palpable waves. Violet longed to hug him and kiss away the shadows that darkened his face. But for her sake and his, she needed to make a clean break—even though giving him up cut her more deeply and more painfully than her attacker's knife ever had.

"That's it then?" he rasped. "You're just going to walk away from what we have?"

"I have to, Gunnar." She drew her bottom lip between her teeth to keep it from quivering. "Until you face your demons and deal with your posttraumatic stress, I can't have you in my life or my sons'."

Gunnar's spine stiffened, and his expression blanked.

"Got it," he growled, then stormed from the room. Down the hall, she heard the door to his room slam shut…and felt her heart break.

Chapter 15

"Want to talk about it?" Emma asked Gunnar quietly as they walked down the sidewalk in the heart of the shopping district of Eden Falls the next morning.

He frowned at his sister. "About what?"

Emma lifted a shoulder. "Whatever's got you in a such bad mood today."

Gunnar clenched his teeth and shot Emma a warning glare. "I'm fine."

The last thing he wanted to do was confess to his nosy sister that he'd found the love of his life, but she wanted nothing to do with him because his head was so screwed up since coming home from Afghanistan.

"Something's wrong," Emma persisted. "Yesterday you were in such a good mood at dinner. You seemed so happy with Violet, and I'd have sworn you two were an item. Then today—"

"Drop it," he grumbled. He glanced ahead of them where Piper gabbed animatedly with Violet as they strolled down the crowded sidewalk. Violet used the crutches Derek had given her to prevent overtaxing her healing leg, but even with the slow pace they were walking, she looked tired.

That morning, Violet had tried to rehash things, begging him to understand why she had to make the choice she had… all while he loaded her suitcases into the ranch's SUV to move her back into town. He understood all he had to. She was leaving. He'd told her he loved her, and she'd rejected him. What else was there to discuss?

Fresh pain raked through his chest.

"Did you two have a fight?" Emma asked.

He squeezed the handles of the bags he carried for Piper and Violet and shot his sister another silencing look. "I said drop it."

Emma scoffed and rolled her eyes. "Don't be

so stubborn, Gunnar! If you care about each other, you can figure something out to make it work. Caleb and I—"

"Emma!" Gunnar stopped walking and took a calming breath, rolling his shoulders to release the mounting tension.

Emma turned when she realized he was no longer beside her and sent him a puzzled look. "All right. Forget I asked. But it's not healthy to keep stuff bottled up. If you don't want to talk to me, talk to Tate or Derek maybe or—"

"I don't want to talk about it," he grated through clenched teeth. "Talking about it just keeps it fresh and raw and festering! Why should I keep reliving it? Why can't you people under-stand that I just want to forget about it!"

Emma's eyes widened. "Whoa. We're not talk-ing about Violet and you having a spat anymore. Are we?"

He growled and scrubbed a hand over his face. Where had that come from?

His sister tipped her head but wisely didn't push for an explanation of his outburst. "Why did you come today if you're in such a bad mood?"

He hoisted the bags and gave her a sarcastic grin. "Someone had to lug Piper's bags around." He lowered his arms and huffed out a breath. He knew he was being an ass, and Emma didn't deserve his churlishness. "Sorry. I don't mean to vent on you."

Cutting a glance down the street, he watched Piper and Violet take a seat at an outdoor table of the café. His chest tightened with regret and loss. "I made a commitment to help protect Violet, and I keep my word. I want to make sure you all don't run into any trouble today from aggressive fans, or paparazzi or…worse."

Not wanting to attract attention in town while they shopped, Violet had worn jeans, an Eden Falls High School sweatshirt of Piper's, no makeup and a baseball cap pulled low over her face. It wasn't much in the way of disguises, but so far no one seemed to have recognized her.

"Okay. I'll back off. But could you try not scowling so much? You're being a real downer."

"I just…" He bit out a curse and shook his head. "I've got a lot of crap to work out, and Violet's leaving brought home to me how hard… how alone…"

Emma laid a hand on his arm. "You're not alone, Gun. You've got your family. You'll always have us, and we love you." She tugged a crooked grin. "Even when you're a grumpy butthead."

He pressed his mouth in a taut line. "I guess I earned that one."

"Mmm-hmm." Emma hitched her head toward the café tables. "Come on. Looks like we're taking a break. You can buy me a mocha latte to make up for snapping at me."

He followed Emma down the sidewalk and piled Piper's purchases in a chair next to the one she'd claimed at the café.

"You don't mind if we grab a snack, do you?" Piper asked Emma as she and Gunnar pulled chairs up to the table. "Violet's leg was hurting, and she wanted to rest a bit before hitting the rest of the shops."

Gunnar sent Violet a hooded glance. They'd barely spoken three words to each other since meeting up with his chatty sisters. The hollow look around her eyes told him she'd slept as poorly last night as he had, but she'd been determined to keep her promise of shopping with Emma and Piper. Later in the morning, they were to meet up with Rani and the twins, and Violet would head back to the B and B that the movie crew was staying at during filming. And he'd likely not see her or the boys again.

I can't have you in my life...

Her feelings couldn't be any plainer than that. He glanced away and feigned interest in the pigeons pecking crumbs near another table, trying hard not to let his sisters or Violet know he was dying inside.

For several minutes, while they all sipped coffee or hot cocoa, Gunnar listened halfheartedly to the ladies chatter about what they were getting Tate, Sawyer or the twins for Christmas. He let his thoughts drift, dreading the coming weeks, the silence that would fill his cabin without Violet and the twins there.

"Gunnar? Hey, Gunnar, did you hear me?" Piper asked.

"What?"

"I asked what you wanted for Christmas." Piper narrowed her eyes and shifted her gaze to look for what had held his attention down the sidewalk. "You okay? You're not going to freak out on us like you did last time we were here, are you?"

Emma frowned. "Freaked out how?"

He turned to Emma. "Never mind." Then to Piper. "No, I'm not going to freak out." Facing Violet, he met the worried expression in her eyes and gritted his teeth. He didn't want her pity. "And I don't want anything for Christmas—nothing that can be bought anyway."

Piper forced a cough while saying, "Scrooge."

"I can't really buy anything for Caleb, either. The Amish don't use most commercial products or exchange store-bought gifts," Emma said, and

Gunnar sipped his coffee, tuning the conversation out as best he could.

"Did you end up buying those driving gloves for Derek?" Violet asked Emma.

"No, but I'm really thinking I should have."

"They were nice gloves," Piper said, "and Mr. Perfect is so hard to buy for. You might as well get the gloves."

"Hmm," Emma said, flattening her hands on the tabletop. "You're right. I think I'll go back and get them." She gathered up the table's empty cups to throw away and scooted her chair back. "You all go on without me. I'll catch up."

"Want to check out the shop next door where the Amish and other local craftsmen sell homemade gifts?" Piper asked Violet. "Gunnar bought the greatest quilt there this summer."

The quilt Violet had worn wrapped around her while they sat on his porch this past week. Gunnar swallowed the grief that rose in him.

"Sure," Violet said, "but we've only got another hour before we're supposed to meet Rani with the boys."

Gunnar's gut pitched. An hour…he only had an hour left to spend with Violet. And he was shopping with his sisters. *Oh, whee,* he thought glumly.

Violet hobbled down the aisle of the gift shop where beautiful Amish-made crafts and the work of other local artisans were sold. She paused, resting her weight on the crutches, as she examined a beaded necklace. In her peripheral vision, she caught a glimpse of Gunnar, shoulders hunched, hands in his pockets, watching her from the next aisle. His brooding silence today spoke for his deep hurt, and she hated that she'd put him in this dark mood.

But she had to protect herself and her boys. Didn't she? Maybe cutting ties with Gunnar was the only thing that would force him to confront the truth about his PTSD and do something to free himself from the ghosts that haunted him. Or maybe she'd only sent him into a deeper depression that would eventually overwhelm him.

A sharp-edged ache constricted her chest, and

she dropped the necklace back on the display. She really wasn't in a mood to Christmas shop, regardless of the promise she'd made Piper. Her leg throbbed, and after tossing and turning most of the night, she was drop-dead tired.

Spying a bench at the back of the store, she headed toward the seat, prepared to wait patiently for Piper. As she limped down the aisle, she passed a magazine rack where a pair of giggling teenage girls flipped through a gossip rag. The photo on the front page stopped her.

Despite Tate and Emma's precautions to guard her privacy, some enterprising photographer had captured an image of Derek's nurse wheeling Violet from the medical clinic two weeks ago. *Injury sidelines Chastain,* the headline read.

Sighing her frustration with the paparazzi, Violet tugged the bill of her cap lower and continued to the back of the store. She kept her chin tucked to her chest, her gaze low as she passed a woman and her husband perusing a display of blown glass, then settled on the bench.

Piper saw her and took a seat beside her. "You okay?"

"Yeah, fine. Just resting a bit until Emma catches up with us. Take your time." She offered the girl an encouraging smile. "There's a lot of great stuff in here."

"Yeah," Piper agreed as her eyes moved to a display beside them and widened. "Like those." She rose from the bench to explore the table full of handmade birdhouses. "Aren't these pretty?"

Violet glanced up long enough to see the colorful houses Piper was admiring. "Very nice."

Behind the table, a man wearing a flannel shirt like a jacket over a white undershirt was painting designs on a birdhouse similar to the ones for sale. When he turned to Piper, Violet ducked her head again, keeping her face largely hidden by the bill of her cap. She followed the exchange between Piper and the craftsman with her gaze fixed on the floor.

"Can I help you?"

"Yeah, maybe. I really like these birdhouses. I'm thinking one of them would make a great present for my sister. She's got an Amish boy-friend and is gonna convert and stuff, so giving her an MP3 player or coffeemaker for Christmas is kinda impractical."

Violet noted that Piper was wearing mis-matched socks and grinned. She'd heard Rani mention this was a popular trend with teenagers.

"Well, the ones at this end are less ornate, so they're more in keeping with Amish tradition." The man shuffled to the end of the table closest to Violet, and she shifted her gaze to his paint-splattered work boots. A tingle nipped Violet at the base of her neck. *Work boots...*

"How much are they?" Piper asked.

"Usually twenty dollars, but for you, pretty lady, half price."

Violet narrowed her eyes on the boots. Why did they cause the flutter of unease to stir in her gut?

Piper's laugh had a coquettish overtone. "Re-ally? That's so nice!"

"Sure thing, sweetheart." Something in the craftsman's tone conjured memories of too many lascivious casting directors she'd known, and Violet shoved aside thoughts of work boots to concentrate on the exchange.

"I'll take that one. Emma will like the flowers on it."

"Good choice. So do you have an Amish boyfriend like your sister?"

None of your business, cretin, Violet thought, growing more uncomfortable with the man's oily tone. Something about the man's voice grated along her nerves and made her squirm.

"Gosh, no. I don't have any boyfriend," Piper said.

"Really? Pretty girl like you?"

Violet gritted her teeth and cast a covert glance to the last place she'd seen Gunnar. If Piper's brother didn't come intervene in this increasingly inappropriate conversation between Piper and a man twice her age soon, Violet was prepared to step in herself. Gunnar was at the newsstand now, studying the picture of her leaving the clinic with a frown denting his brow.

As if feeling her stare, Gunnar glanced her

way, and Violet held eye contact with him while hitching her head toward Piper.

He frowned in query, then shrugged and turned to put the gossip rag back on the news-stand.

The teenagers who had been giggling by the news rack earlier walked past Violet, and she dropped her chin to her chest again, shifting her attention back to Piper's and the craftsman's shoes.

"My brother teases me about being tall for a girl," Piper said.

"I like tall girls," the sleezoid craftsman said.

Violet had heard enough. Forsaking the crutches, she struggled to her feet and stepped closer to the table of birdhouses. "Back off, buddy. She's a minor, and you're old enough to—"

The end of her tirade lodged in her throat when the man faced her. In the space of seconds, his expression shifted from irritation to startled rec-ognition. A heartbeat later, his face registered in Violet's memory.

She gasped and staggered back a step. Her brain clicked as the pieces fell into place—paint-splattered work boots, his voice, the police sketch...

"Y-you're..." she rasped but got no further.

As the man's expression hardened, he plowed his way around the table of birdhouses, knocking past Piper, and bolted for the front door.

Violet ignored the pain in her leg and, with a limping jog, pursued the man up an aisle of jewelry. "No! Gunnar, that's him! The kidnapper! Stop him!"

Gunnar jerked his head up. His gaze found Violet first, then the man fleeing to the front door. Sprinting to the end of the aisle, Gunnar stepped between the man and his escape route. He blocked the fleeing man with a classic football stance and a shoulder to the guy's ribs.

The force of Gunnar's tackle sent the man staggering back several steps and crashing into a display of polished rocks.

"Charlie! What's going on?" the woman be-hind the register asked, her voice nervous.

The man—Charlie, the woman had called him—kept his focus on Gunnar. "Outta my way, man."

"No." Gunnar sized the guy up. He could take him. Easily. The guy was big, but Gunnar had three inches and thirty pounds of muscle on him. He edged closer to Charlie, ready to engage him if needed. But some backup would be nice.

Charlie's gaze darted around the store, the frantic look of a trapped animal in his eyes. "I said move!"

What was taking Emma so long to buy those damn gloves? Without taking his eyes off Char-lie, Gunnar shouted to the woman, "Call the po-lice!"

The man reached behind him under his flannel shirt and drew a gun he'd had tucked at the small of his back. "No police! No phones!" He made a quick swipe of his arm around the room. "I want every cell phone brought up here. Now!" When the customers only gaped at him in shock, Charlie fired the gun once into the ceiling. "Now!"

The teenage girls screamed and scampered to drop their phones at his feet.

Gunnar figured his best move, unarmed as he was, was to keep the gunman as calm as possible until Emma and her service weapon arrived. *Appease the guy, until he lowers his guard and you can make your move.*

"Okay," Gunnar said, raising his hands, then pulled his phone from the clip at his belt and slid it across the floor. "Do what he asked, Piper."

Her face pale with fear, Piper followed suit then scuttled close to Gunnar. The cashier glared at Charlie, then tossed her phone next to the others. The older couple who had been milling around the store used the moment of distraction to dart out the front door. Charlie saw the pair hustle out and grew agitated. "Damn it, no one leaves unless I do!"

Violet edged toward the front of the store, her hands up to show they were empty. "There's no need to hurt anyone. Please, just put the gun down."

"Shut up!" Charlie whirled, aiming the weapon at Violet's chest.

Ice streaked through Gunnar's veins, and a cold sweat popped out on his lip. The image of broken, bleeding bodies scattered around the Afghan marketplace flashed in his mind's eye. He shook his head once and blinked hard to clear his head. *Keep it together. Violet and Piper need you.*

"This is your fault!" Charlie shouted at Violet.

Anxiety knotting his gut, Gunnar leaned toward Piper. "Get Violet, and move behind something solid. Don't come out until I tell you."

Gunnar's whisper dragged Charlie's attention back to him. "What are you doing?"

"Just telling her to take cover. I don't want her hurt...and neither do you." Gunnar eased forward, his tone calm, his hands up. "Why don't you hand me the gun?"

Charlie laughed bitterly. "Like hell. Why don't

you step aside and let me out of here before I put a bullet in your brain?"

Violet gasped. "Gunnar, please. Don't push him…"

"You should listen to the lady." Charlie closed in on Gunnar, the weapon in his hand shaking. Gunnar knew a green, jumpy soldier was a trigger-happy soldier. An animal was most dangerous when cornered. But he'd be damned if he'd let this man who'd attacked Violet, who'd kidnapped Amish girls for a sex ring, get past him and go free.

Charlie made a move toward the door, and Gunnar leaped, swinging an arm with an upward arc to knock the man's gun hand up, then tackled him.

"Gunnar!" Piper cried.

His momentum knocked Charlie to the floor, and Gunnar grappled with his opponent for control of the gun. In the melee of wrenched arms and flying fists, the weapon discharged. A blown glass vase over their heads shattered.

Using his superior strength and size, Gunnar

gained the upper hand and slammed the man's gun hand to the floor until the weapon skittered away. Seizing his chance, Gunnar released Charlie and pounced on the gun. He snatched the weapon up and spun back to face the other man, aiming for Charlie's heart.

But Charlie wasn't ready to concede defeat. He staggered to his feet, panting and snarling at Gunnar. "You won't shoot me. You don't have the guts."

Gunnar narrowed his eyes and angled his head. "I pulled the trigger way more than once in my five tours in Afghanistan."

Uncertainty flickered across the man's face. Tensing, Charlie jerked his gaze down the aisle where Violet watched the events with apprehensive eyes.

As quickly as the man's intent registered in Gunnar's mind, Charlie had grabbed Violet and yanked her in front of him as a shield. She yelped in fear and pain as her injured leg buckled.

"Let her go!" Gunnar growled, hearing the note of panic in his voice. Sucking in a deep breath, Gunnar fought for composure despite the turn of events. He couldn't reveal his fear for Violet or Charlie could use it against him.

"No." Charlie snaked an arm around Violet's throat and another around her waist, lifting her from the floor as if she were a rag doll. "You weren't the only one who served in the military. Uncle Sam taught me how to break someone's neck with one twist. You slide me the gun and let me pass, or the pretty lady dies."

She couldn't breathe. Violet kicked her legs, desperate for leverage to relieve the pressure of the kidnapper's arm across her throat. The man's threat to snap her neck chilled her to the bone, and adrenaline fueled her struggle. But the man's viselike hold was unyielding.

Air. She needed air.

She's played the victim of crime in plenty of movies, but living such terror in reality was a different beast. Already her vision was growing fuzzy. She had to have oxygen soon or…

"Let. Her. Go." Gunnar's command was a steely and cold as his expression.

Despite the stony warrior expression he wore, she saw the Gunnar who'd laughed and played gently with her boys. She saw the compassionate man who'd opened his home to her and doted on her as she convalesced. She saw…spots.

Oh, God…was she flashing on those aspects of Gunnar because she was dying? Was this her brain reliving the sweet moments at the end?

"Drop the gun," her captor snarled in return. She wouldn't survive a prolonged standoff, a testosterone-infused battle of wills between the men. She clawed at Charlie's hands, gasping for air.

Without warning, Charlie shifted his grip on her. He moved his arm from her neck to circle her head and sink his fingers into the side of her forehead.

With a ragged gulp, Violet sucked in precious air, the influx of oxygen making her dizzy. As grateful as she was to breathe, two stark truths jolted her like current from a Taser.

One, she loved Gunnar and couldn't bear to give him up. And two, Charlie's new grip gave him perfect leverage to snap her neck.

Gunnar's heart thundered, and his pulse pounded in his ears. He'd played deadly games of chicken before without blinking...and won. But he'd never had someone he loved caught in the middle. How could he risk Violet's life?

"Get out of my way or blondie dies," Charlie grated.

Gunnar's gut told him Charlie was bluffing, that he was just desperate, and if he kept him talking, kept him occupied until Emma arrived—damn it, Emma, what was taking so long to buy one pair of gloves?—he could help bring in one of the creeps involved in the kidnapping ring. But what if his gut was wrong? What if he failed? What if he screwed this up and he lost someone he loved?

Again the image of the dead Afghan boy from the street market crowded into his mind, distracting him. His hand shook harder, and his gut pitched. *You let that boy down and he died,* a voice in his head taunted.

No, no, no! Not now! Gunnar shook his head, blinked hard, forcibly erasing the voice, the image from his head. If he lost focus, if he let the ghosts of the marketplace bombing get in his head now, Violet could die.

Acid roiled in his stomach, and he gritted his teeth as he redirected his attention to Charlie. Get him to talk…

Keeping the gun trained on Charlie, Gunnar raised one hand in a conciliatory gesture. He cut a furtive glance to Piper, who'd rounded up the other teenage girls and hunkered down behind a sturdy display case. *Good girl.* "C'mon, man. You don't want to add murder charges to anything you've already done."

Charlie's feet shifted, his eyes darting to the front door, then back to Gunnar. "I'll kill her if I have to. I will!"

"You don't have to. If you talk, if you give them names and locations, I'd bet you can get a deal. A good deal." The thought of this guy cutting a deal and getting away with attacking Violet made Gunnar nauseated, but he took a breath and forged on. "What happened to the girl who was with Violet last week?"

Charlie shook his head, and he swallowed hard, making his Adam's apple bob. "I don't know. My job is just to get the girls."

"For who?" Gunnar made sure to keep his voice flat, calm, even though chaos ruled his insides.

"I don't know their names. They run an on-line dating service for guys who like…virgins."

Dating service, my ass. Gunnar clenched his jaw tighter and swallowed the bile that rose in his throat. While Charlie talked, he crept a small step closer to Violet.

"What did they pay you for getting the girls?"

A sheen of perspiration had popped out on Charlie's face, and he nervously shifted his stance again. "It's not like that! I wouldn't do it if I didn't have to!"

"Have to?" Gunnar heard the hard edge in his

tone and mentally checked himself. *Stay cool.* He moved closer to Violet and her captor.

"Hey! Stay back!" Charlie snarled, lunging back a few steps and dragging Violet stumbling with him. Her injured leg buckled, and she cried out in pain.

Adrenaline spiked in Gunnar's blood, and the screams and dying moans of the bombing aftermath echoed in his head. *Your friends died because of your mistake!* Shaking to his core, Gunnar battled down the memory of broken bodies and lifeless eyes. He couldn't lose control of this situation. He had to rein in the burgeoning flashback, keep his head.

"I owed them money. I…used their services once and…they hiked up the fees after I brought the girl back."

Gunnar dragged his attention to Charlie, fighting the rage and panic and guilt that clawed at him.

"I couldn't pay, and they…they said they'd take payment another way." His face crumpled, and his voice cracked. "They knew I have a fifteen-year-old daughter. They said they'd take her if I didn't help them bring in Amish girls."

Gunnar struggled to calm his ragged breathing.

Keep him talking. Buy time. "Wh-who are they?"

Charlie's face contorted in a feral snarl. "I said I don't know! No names were used!"

Violet gasped, winced, and Gunnar saw Charlie's grip on her tighten as he lifted her feet from the floor once more. Damn it! Charlie *had* already said that he didn't know who he was working for. *Stay in the game. Concentrate. Focus!* If his distraction led to Violet's death...he'd want to die himself.

"Okay," Gunnar said, his voice thick. He inhaled. Exhaled. "Okay. You were protecting your daughter. I get that. You had your reasons for taking the Amish girl. I'd do the same thing." *Yeah, when hell froze over.* "Why don't you let Violet go now, and we can talk some more—"

"No!" Charlie took his hand off Violet's head

and aimed an accusing finger at Gunnar. "No more stalling! Get the hell out of my way!"

Violet twisted in Charlie's grasp, and when her toes found purchase with the floor, she used the leverage to throw her head back into Charlie's nose. She followed with a swift jab of her elbow in his gut and spun away from his startled and weakened grip.

"Bitch!" Charlie growled and swiped a hand through the air, groping for Violet.

Gunnar tensed, his finger curling around the trigger.

Violet ran a step, then cried out and fell, holding her leg, clearing Gunnar's shot.

Training kicked in, and in the next heartbeat, Gunnar aimed and squeezed the trigger.

The blast reverberated through him. Female screams filled the air. Violet lay motionless on the floor. For a second that lasted an eternity, Gunnar feared he'd hit Violet.

"FBI! Nobody move!" Emma shouted as she burst through the front door of the shop.

Gunnar sucked in a shaky breath and held it. *Violet!* Why wasn't she moving?

Emma's gaze swept the room, taking a quick mental inventory before zeroing in on Charlie, who groaned and clutched his thigh. "Show me your hands, buddy! Slowly." Her gun trained on the kidnapper, Emma moved forward. "Violet? Are you okay?"

A post-adrenaline crash sent a wave of tremors and nausea rolling through Gunnar. He staggered toward Violet and dropped to his knees beside her. "Violet?"

She rolled to her back and blinked at him with frightened doe eyes. "Breath. Knocked. From… me," she gasped, and only then did Gunnar take a breath himself.

He stroked the side of her face, his hand trembling. "Are you hurt?"

She shook her head and clutched his hand as she dragged in thin gasps. Gunnar helped her sit up, then pulled her onto his lap to hold her, to reassure himself she was safe, to calm the tumult still jangling inside him. "Oh, God, Tink.

I was so scared he'd hurt you. If something had happened to you—"

"I'm…all right." She buried her face in his shoulder and clung to him, her body racked with tremors.

Emma pulled a pair of handcuffs from under her windbreaker and snapped them on Charlie's wrist. When Emma rolled Charlie to his back, Gunnar spotted the bloody wound on the man's thigh.

Payback, he thought with smug satisfaction. *We'll see how he likes having a hole in his leg like the one he gave Violet.*

"Piper?" Emma called as she snatched a decorative scarf from a display and shoved it against the seeping wound on Charlie's leg.

The teen surged to her feet and ran to Emma. "I thought you'd never get here!"

"Piper, call an ambulance and the local police and get them in here," Emma said brusquely. "This is their jurisdiction until we *officially* tie this guy to the kidnappings."

Piper scuttled over to the pile of cell phones Charlie had collected and found hers.

"And good job leaving an open line to me," Emma added, her tone softening for her little sister. "Smart thinking. I heard everything."

Gunnar looked up. "What did Piper do?"

Piper joined them again but kept Emma between her and Charlie. "When I tossed my phone on the pile, I hit the key to speed-dial Emma's cell."

"When I answered, I heard the shouting and knew there was trouble," Emma said while applying pressure to Charlie's wound.

Violet smiled at Piper. "Smart."

Emma glared at Charlie, who was groaning in pain. "By the way, you have the right to say nothing now, until you have a lawyer present." The tinkle of the bell over the front door drew Emma's gaze, and she shouted to the teenage girls who were trying to leave. "Hold up there, ladies. You need to stay and give the police a statement. Lock that door, and have a seat at the back of the store."

"Wow." Gunnar sent Emma a half grin, his pulse finally settling back in a normal rhythm. "Look at Tomato-head taking control of the situation."

Emma sent him a smug look. "Don't sound so surprised." Her expression modulated, and she lifted one auburn eyebrow. "You didn't do so bad handling the situation yourself. Good job, big bro."

Gunnar forced a quick grin and jerked a nod of acknowledgment, but his gut rebelled with sour disgust. Emma didn't know the truth, didn't know how close he'd been to a meltdown, didn't know how his fear for Violet's life had almost paralyzed him.

Violet smoothed a hand down one cheek and placed a warm kiss on the other. "My hero."

Her adulation raked through him with sharp tines. He was anything but a hero.

When the room seemed to shrink around him, he shoved to his feet, helping Violet up as he did so, then set her away from him. "I'll be back. I…I need air."

"Gunnar?" Violet and Emma called after him.

But he didn't stop. His personal demons had put Piper and Violet in jeopardy today, and that was unacceptable. Whatever it took, he would take control of this…this…

Posttraumatic stress disorder. He sighed and admitted the truth to himself. He needed help to take control of his life again—before it was too late.

The hour grew late before the Eden Falls police had finished questioning everyone about the incident in the crafts store. Violet called Rani and told her to keep the twins at the bed-and-breakfast until she could get free to meet them. After they had all answered questions for the police report, Gunnar and Emma had insisted she go to Derek's clinic, just to make sure she was all right. She had some bruising on her throat from Charlie's choke hold and a few scrapes from tussling with him, but she was alive…thanks to Gunnar. She had no doubt his quick thinking and courage to take on the kidnapper, facing down the man's gun, had saved her life today.

Violet wanted desperately to have some time alone with Gunnar, to thank him for his heroics and to tell him some of the things she'd realized about their relationship today. But Gunnar had disappeared from his brother's clinic as soon as Derek passed on a good report on her.

With a heavy and troubled heart, she returned to the bed-and-breakfast, eager to hug her children after her brush with death. What would have happened to Hudson and Mason if she had been killed? Her family would have taken them in, of course, but she hated to think of her babies growing up without a mother or father.

Her thoughts flashed again to Gunnar playing with her boys, laughing with them, hugging them when they cried. Gunnar was nothing like Adam, whose self-involved lifestyle and self-destructive addiction had taken him from his children and caused her heartache. She saw that so clearly now. And she also saw that she'd cast Gunnar's issues with PTSD in the same category as Adam's drug problem when they were so different. She'd been scared, confused by her feelings for him. She'd overreacted. She'd been unfair.

That evening when she went to bed in her room at the B and B, she tried to called Gunnar, but he didn't answer his cell. While she stared down at the phone in her hand, it jangled her incoming call tones, and her heart leaped.

"Hello?" she said, full of hope.

"Violet, it's Emma. I promised to call you when I had news."

"Oh, hi." Violet tried to hide the disappointment in her tone.

"Charlie cut a deal. He'll still do time, but he gave up his partner. That's probably not a lot of comfort to you but…it's something."

"No, no, that's good. Did he say anything that will help you find Mary and the other girls?" Violet stroked Sophie's fur when the cat jumped up on the bed and settled in next to her.

"I can't get into classified details of the case but…we do have a few tentative leads." Emma went on to explain the kidnapper, Charlie Harris, was a farmer from a nearby community who built birdhouses and other wood crafts to sell on the weekends at the Eden Falls store. He had no priors other than parking tickets and a domestic disturbance call that happened just before his divorce. Once treated for the gunshot wound in his leg, he was interrogated by the police in his hospital room.

His accomplice was another lackey for hire being threatened by the men behind the online sex ring. Harris swore he had nothing that could identify the men who now held Mary Yoder and the other girls. He claimed that after he and his partner grabbed the girls, they handed them off to a third man, described only as medium height, dark-haired and mean-looking, on an isolated side road in the heart of Amish country.

"Violet, we will do everything in our power to find Mary and bring her home. I promise," Emma said, and the steel edge in her voice told Violet just how serious Emma was in her intent. After all, Caleb Troyer's sister was among the missing girls. For Emma, as for Violet, this case was personal.

"Thank you, Emma. For everything." Violet closed her eyes and sighed. "Will you do one other favor for me? If you see Gunnar, tell him I need to talk to him."

"Will do. Good night."

Violet disconnected the call with her thumb and let her hand fall limply to the bed. She was both physically and mentally exhausted.

"And I need to talk to you, too," a familiar voice said from her door.

Violet sat up with a jerk, whipping her gaze to the ruggedly handsome man across the room. "Gunnar."

"Hi. I was worried about you after what happened today. How are you?" His gaze drifted to the bruises darkening on her neck, and a scowl tugged his mouth down.

She pulled the collar of her bathrobe up to hide the distracting evidence of her injury. "Shaken, but...relieved that Harris has been caught." She frowned. "Even if it doesn't bring the cops any closer to finding Mary."

He lifted a shoulder. "You'd be surprised how little tips and pieces of information can lead to a big picture and arrests. Emma and Tate will catch the scum behind the sex ring. Have faith."

"You wanted to talk?" she asked at the same time he said, "What did you want to—?"

Then together, "You first."

They both grinned awkwardly and shook their heads. Gunnar moved from the door to the corner of her bed in the few silent seconds that followed and gave Sophie a quick scratch behind her ears.

Violet took a deep breath. Perhaps it was best that she go first.

"I was wrong," she said, as he blurted, "You were right."

Violet chuckled and raked fingers through her hair before his statement hit her. "What?"

"Today I realized—" he started, then paused as if making sure he had the floor "—you were right. All of you. Derek, Emma, Tate, even Piper…

you've all told me at some point since I came home from the war that I need help. I need to see a counselor. And you were right. I saw that today, and…this afternoon, I called a counselor in Philly that the army recommended."

Violet pressed a hand to her mouth as tears of joy and relief prickled her sinuses.

"I start biweekly sessions with him on Monday." He met her eyes with the soul-piercing gaze that had reached deep inside her from the day they met. "I just wanted you to know that."

She moved her hand to his forearm and squeezed. "Oh, Gunnar, I'm so glad. This is the right thing. But…what changed your mind?"

He shifted his gaze to stare at the floor, a deep furrow in his brow. "The way things went down today. Things could have turned out so differently if—" His Adam's apple dipped as he swallowed, and he raised tortured eyes to her. "If something had happened to you because I'd lost control of the situation, lost control over…" He paused, drawing a shaky breath, and Violet bit her lip, giving him time to say his piece, determined not to rush him.

"I started having another flashback...when he pulled the gun. When he threatened you and I thought I could lose you—" another pause, another deep breath "—I had to fight the memories, fight my fears with all my strength. I realized if I let the flashback take control of me, my mind, I'd lose control of the situation. It finally clicked that I'd been letting my nightmares, my...PTSD...control me and my entire existence for months."

Gunnar rubbed a hand over his face and got up to pace the room. "I'm living like a hermit. I'm grumpy and withdrawn...just like my family has been telling me. I want my life back."

Violet's heart warmed hearing the revelations Gunnar had made. He was far from cured, but his acceptance of his condition, his desire to get better and change his life meant so much. She smiled as he continued, clearly on a roll as he enumerated his hopes for the future.

"I want...to get involved with my parents'

charity and volunteer in the community. I want to go to bed at night without fearing the nightmares. I want to spend time with Sawyer and Piper without worrying if I'm going to have another breakdown in front of them. I want a family. I want—" he stopped abruptly and jerked his head up, his anxious gaze darting to hers "—I want you, Violet. You and the boys."

Her breath stuck in her lungs, and a hot flash of adrenaline swept through her. She gaped at him, unable to speak around the knot of emotions in her throat.

He rushed over to her and took her hands in his. "I know what you said yesterday. I know Adam and his addiction hurt you. And I honestly didn't come tonight to try to change your mind, but—"

She shook her head rapidly, battling down the clog in her throat, needed to let him know the revelations she'd had. "No. No, Gunnar, I—"

"I understand your reasons for wanting me out of your life," he interrupted, adding in a rush, "I know you don't want to repeat the crap

Adam put you through. I know we're different. I know we've been over all the reasons why we could never work. I'm not trying to change your mind—"

"You're not?" Violet's heart sank. Did her selfish, frightened ultimatum last night mean she'd lost her chance with Gunnar?

"I know you're doing what's right for you and the boys. I won't stop you from walking away. I just wanted you to know—"

She squeezed his hands. Hard. "*You're* what's right for us."

"I meant what I said. I love you. I love the boys. I want to—" He blinked. "What?"

She smiled her apology as tears leaked onto her cheeks. "I was wrong to push you out of my life. You aren't Adam. His addiction made him selfish and distant. These past two weeks, despite everything you've been dealing with— your nightmares, being pressed into service as a nurse and babysitter, paparazzi trespassing on your land—you've been nothing but kind and protective and helpful. You've been a better father to my boys in two weeks than Adam was in the eight months he had with them."

"Tink, I—"

"No, it's my turn. Let me finish, okay?"

Gunnar jerked a nod, a curious wrinkle denting his brow.

"Adam chose the drugs, chose to ignore the warning signs our marriage was suffering, chose to cheat on me. He chose the path that led to his death. You didn't do anything but serve your country and witness horrors no one should. I respect your service and sacrifice, and walking away from you because of what those horrors did to you would be wrong."

Gunnar's face darkened. "I don't want pity. I'm not a charity case."

"No! Of course not! But your situation is so different from Adam's, I…I can't believe I couldn't see how selfish I was being."

He opened his mouth again, and she covered his lips with her hand. "The fact that you recognize your need for help puts you miles ahead and far apart from Adam in so many ways. And

before I miss my chance, I want you to know…
I love you, too, and I want to give us a chance."

The tension beneath her fingers fell away, and his eyes warmed, dampened. "You do? Really?"

She nodded, fresh tears spilling from her lashes.

Gunnar reached for her, jamming his hand through her hair to catch the back of her head. He drew her close and captured her lips in a kiss that was deep and sweet and full of heart. Violet wrapped her arms around his neck and clung to him, her hope soaring.

"Mommy!" Mason's squeal was followed by the thud of two sets of running feet.

Violet pulled reluctantly from Gunnar's kiss and greeted the twins as they clambered up on her bed, sending Sophie running for cover.

"Nunnar!" Hudson said, throwing himself against Gunnar for a hug.

"Hey, buddy!" Gunnar gave each of the boys a hug of genuine and mutual affection.

And she knew in her soul she was making the right decision.

Rani appeared at the door and gasped. "Oh, I'm sorry. I didn't know you had company. I told them they could get you for story time and prayers."

"No problem. In fact, will you give us a few minutes alone with them?" Violet said, wincing as Mason hugged her sore neck a bit too tight.

"Sure. Call if you need me." Rani backed out of the room and closed the door.

"C'mere, pal." Seeing her predicament, Gunnar tugged Mason closer and redirected her toddler's attention. "Why don't you go pick out a book over there while I talk to your mommy. Okay?" He pointed to the stack of books on the floor by their reading pillow.

"'Kay," Mason chirped and climbed down, Hudson following.

Gunnar faced her again, and his expression grew grave. "What were you saying about giving us a chance?"

"I want what you want. A family. A future with you."

He gave her a skeptical frown. "What about all the differences in our lifestyles?"

"Frankly..." She lifted a corner of her mouth. "I'd love to spend a few months every year in a quiet cabin, alone with my boys and...you. I already planned to be more selective about what roles I take so I could spend more quality time with the twins. The question is, could you be happy spending part of the year in Hollywood or wherever I'm filming? Having the media watching your every public move?"

Gunnar flashed a lopsided grin. "Let them watch. I'll be the envy of every man in America having you on my arm." He kissed her hand. "I can handle the paparazzi if you can. Which reminds me, if you still need a date to the SAG Awards, I'm available."

Violet grinned. "And the Golden Globes? And the Oscars?"

"Sign me up."

She smiled, then sobered. "Are you sure? Being a public figure is a crazy life. I want you to be sure about this."

He drew her close and brushed a kiss on her lips. "Very sure. I want to be with you, Tink. I want to make a family with you and the boys and…maybe a couple more kids. I want to be at your side to protect you and honor you and watch your star shine. We'll deal with the crazy stuff public life throws us, and I promise to deal with my PTSD and not let it control me anymore."

Happiness bloomed in her chest, filling her and bubbling up in a laugh of delight. "Sounds like a plan."

Sophie had just resettled at the foot of the bed when the boys returned.

"This one!" Mason slapped a book on Gunnar's lap before Hudson shoved his brother aside and dropped his choice of book on top of Mason's.

"No, mine!"

Violet gave her nervous-looking cat a calming pet.

"Easy, son. We have time to read both." As Mason crawled up beside Violet, Gunnar lifted Hudson onto his lap and scooted close to her.

He sent her a crooked smile that made her pulse scamper and her spirits soar. "We have all the time in the world."

* * * * *